Witch Mirror?

A WATER WITCH MYSTERY
BOOK FIVE

LEAH R CUTTER

KNOTTED ROAD PRESS

Witch Mirror?
A Water Witch Mystery
Book 5
Copyright © 2025 Leah Cutter
All rights reserved
Published by Knotted Road Press
www.KnottedRoadPress.com

Cover Art:
GetCovers.com

ISBN: 978-1-64470-431-8

Cover and interior design copyright © 2025 Knotted Road Press
http://www.KnottedRoadPress.com

Reviews
It's true. Reviews help me sell more books. If you've enjoyed this story, please consider leaving a review of it on your favorite site.

Come someplace new...
Do you enjoy exploring strange new worlds, new cultures, new people?

Sign up for my newsletter and I'll start you on your travels with a free copy of my book, *The Island Sampler*.

http://www.LeahCutter.com/newsletter/

Buy More!
Did you know that you can buy directly from the Knotted Road Press website?

https://www.knottedroadpress.com/shop/

Mysteries

The Water Witch Mysteries

The Witch is Inn

To Scratch a Witch

Witches and Waterways

Grilled Sand and Witches

Witch Mirror?

The Lake Hope Cozy Mysteries

The Purloined Letter Opener

The Tell Tale Heart Pin

The Halley Brown PI Mysteries

Dancer in Darkness

Trophy Hunters

Collections

The Alvin Goodfellow Case Files

The Rabbit Mysteries

The Shredded Veil Mysteries

Magazine

Mystery, Crime, and Mayhem

War Among the Crocodiles

The Cassie Stories

Poisoned Pearls

Tainted Waters

Spoiled Harvest

Bloodied Ice

Epic Fantasy Series

The Fallen Elves

Ruins of the Gods

Stairs of the Gods

Cities of the Gods

Graves of the Gods

Houses of the Dead

Houses Divided

Houses Fallen

Houses Reborn

Forgotten Gods

A Wind Blown Torment

A Stone Strewn Clash

A Sea Washed Victory

The Tanesh Empire Trilogy

The Glass Magician

The Desert Heart

The Ghost Dog

Science Fiction

The Long Run

Project Nemesis

Project Nyx

Project Tisiphone

Project Persephone

War of the Allied Worlds

The Labors of Darius Linard

Huli Intergalactic: Science/Space Fantasy

Origins

The Strawberry Girl

Introduction

Welcome to the fifth (FIFTH!) book in the Water Witch mystery series.

I never anticipated writing this many books in a single series. And the sixth is already vaguely planned out. When the time is right I'll write the next one.

I've grown to love AJ, Bea, and the small town of Milltown, with its quirky characters. And I love writing these books as well.

Every book I write has its own rhythm. The Water Witch mysteries all have a snappy cycle that goes like this:

- Comment
- Reply
- Eyeroll

That's part of what makes these books so much fun for me to write, because AJ has opinions about everything. And everyone. And yes, if I ever met her in person, she'd probably have opinions about me as well.

There are a couple of tarot card readings in this book. (When I did a Kickstarter for the first three novels, I offered tarot card readings for people who participated. In the Kickstarter edition, I also included written out tarot card readings.)

I have done tarot card readings since I was a pre-teen. I still have my first deck, a Rider-Waite deck that I keep in a black velvet bag that I sewed when I first got them.

What's fun about the readings in this book is that the cards that I describe were actually what I drew when I started writing those particular sections. I didn't make them up, or just decide that these were the appropriate cards. I drew them from the deck, in that order.

Do I believe in tarot cards? AJ actually expresses my feeling about them in this book, namely, that the cards are loaded with symbols. Our brains pick out symbols more readily than words. So the words aren't as important, the symbols are already doing the work for the reader.

Or something like that.

I hope that you enjoy this addition to the Water Witch mysteries. Sign up for my newsletter if you want to learn when the next one is coming out!

https://www.leahcutter.com/newsletter/

Cheers!
Leah R Cutter
March 2025
Ravensdale, WA

Chapter One

AJ pulled herself out of the refreshing pool and sauntered over to the long lounge chair holding her towel. She flopped down on her stomach with a happy sigh, the sunlight warming her after the cool water. Despite it being the second week of September, the temperatures were in the mid-70s during the days, though returning to pleasantly cool in the evenings.

A finger poked AJ's arm.

She ignored it.

The poke happened a second, then a third time.

"What?" AJ said, exasperated, as she lifted her head and glared at her younger sister Bea.

Bea sat up on a lounger similar to AJ's. However, instead of a swimsuit like a *normal* person would put on when going to a pool, Bea was completely covered, head to toe. A loose, floral, long-sleeved blouse protected her top half, while equally loose long pants did the same thing for her bottom half. She wore a large brimmed hat with her blonde curls tucked all up inside. Plus she sat under an umbrella.

No sunlight would dare corrupt her sister's perfectly white skin.

"Did you put on sunscreen?" Bea asked primly.

"Yes," AJ said.

"When?"

"Thirty minutes before I went into the water, to give it a chance to adhere," AJ said. "And yes, it's waterproof."

"Well, you should put on more," Bea said. "Particularly if you're going to be tempting fate by just lying there."

AJ sighed, no longer relaxed and enjoying herself. "I will put more on," she promised. "After I've dried off. Only if that will get you off my back."

"The chances of skin cancer—" Bea started.

"Aren't great. There is no cancer in our family line," AJ cut her off. "We die of heart attacks. Not cancer."

Bea pouted at her.

AJ rolled her eyes, grabbed a second towel and dried off a little before she handed the sunscreen to her sister. "Here. Get my back."

"What, it's spray on?" Bea asked.

"Mod cons, you know?" AJ shot back. "Those modern conveniences. Whatever will they think of next? Sliced bread?"

"Funny," Bea said as she sprayed probably three times as much sunscreen as AJ actually needed onto her back.

"Happy, Mom?" AJ said as she took the can back and applied some to her front.

Bea glared in response.

"Speaking of Mom, is she still inside?" AJ asked, gesturing toward the resort that rose up beside the mostly empty pool area.

"Yeah, she said it was a business call," Bea said.

"Business? Really?" AJ said, surprised. "Not one of her charities?"

Bea shrugged.

The idea of a "girls' getaway" had been their mother's. She was having some work done on the house she'd bought in Milltown, and had needed to oversee it while it was ongoing. So she couldn't stay at her house, and hadn't wanted to bother either AJ or Bea, even though Bea had a nice guestroom she could use. Instead, Mom had rented the three of them a luxury condo at one of the coastal resorts, just up the coast from Milltown, and they were vacationing there for a couple of days.

So here AJ was, on a Tuesday afternoon, relaxing by a pool with her sister. Without their mother.

"Think she'll be finished soon?" AJ said as she lowered herself back down on her towel, preparing to soak up as much heat and sun as she could. Fall rains were just around the corner. She was very happy to spend the last few nice days outside.

"Who knows?" Bea said, sounding annoyed.

AJ glanced up at Bea, who held an open book in one hand. She deliberately waited until Bea had started reading again before she spoke up.

"Whatcha reading?"

Bea glared at AJ over the top of the book. "Unauthorized biography of Damien Hirst, the artist."

AJ glanced at the cover of the book, which was covered in colorful small dots. "Abstracts?" she guessed.

"You got it," Bea said, giving her a grin. Bea's own paintings were frequently abstracts, though usually done in a style called boho-chic. She made a lot of money with her art, and had something of a reputation herself, which sometimes surprised AJ.

AJ just shook her head. "Way too sophisticated for the likes of me."

Bea just snorted. "Me as well. But he does have an interesting style…"

AJ closed her eyes and continued to relax, letting the warm sunlight melt her bones into taffy.

Light shone against her closed eyelids.

Now what?

AJ opened her eyes and turned her head to glare at Bea.

But Bea sat in her chair, absorbed in her book, not looking at AJ. Not bothering her at all. Unless she had a flashlight hidden away in one of those voluminous sleeves…

"Hello, dears!" came the call of their mother.

"Hey, ya," AJ said, pushing herself up so she could wave at their mother coming into the pool area.

"Sorry, that took longer than I thought it would," Mom said, nodding as she came over with her own bag and towels. She dragged another long lounger over beside where the girls were and flopped down herself, under the same shady umbrella that Bea used.

Mom looked good, as always. She was shorter than AJ, with the same sort of slim build and dark hair, though hers had a few artistically placed white strands running through it. She'd earned the few wrinkles and laugh lines in her face being in her late sixties, and always felt like a whirlwind of energy, even when she was supposedly on vacation. She wore a smart one-piece bathing suit that was probably a one-of-a-kind designer piece, primarily black with large green leaves and pink tropical flowers decorating it.

"You working on another big charity event?" AJ asked.

Mom gave her a toothy grin. "Oh, something better than

that." She peered more closely at AJ. "Did you put on sunscreen?"

Bea snorted and AJ rolled her eyes. "Yes, Mom, I did. Mom number two sitting over there made sure of it."

"Good. I know you don't take care of your skin like you should, what with swimming in the ocean and all, but even just a little care could make all the difference in the world. Why, I bet it would take five years or more off your appearance!"

AJ rolled her eyes, shook her head, then flopped back down onto her lounge chair again, determined to not let either her mom or her little sister bug her anymore.

However, when she closed her eyes, the light was back, shining against her lids.

What the heck?

AJ opened her eyes and realized with a sinking feeling that the water of the pool had a strong glittering shine to it, as though a hidden spotlight was bouncing its beam on it.

A familiar urge followed immediately, pulling her forward, as if water had been wrapped around her and now the tide was going out quickly.

Crap.

She was about to have a vision.

A big one, too, if the amount of glare and the strength of the urge pulling her forward were anything to go by.

AJ worked her jaw, trying to get out the words as she slipped off the lounger and sat her butt down on the hot cement.

"Vision," she croaked out.

Bea was at her side in an instant. "We're here. We got you."

The words sounded very far away as AJ was tugged under the waves.

Chapter Two

A mirror stood in front of AJ. Tall and oval, with a simple wooden frame. A cheval, if she was remembering correctly. The ceiling above her came to a high peak and she could only stand up straight in the center of the space. Was she in a loft? Maybe. She really couldn't see that much past the mirror.

A very attractive young man appeared in the mirror. His tanned skin highlighted his amber eyes. Blond hair—almost white—tipped the edges of his shaggy cut. He gave her a sexy, *come hither* smile.

AJ snorted. He was at least twenty years younger than AJ, which put him in his early twenties. If that.

A noose suddenly materialized around his neck and jerked him to the side, out of sight. The empty mirror looked gray and cloudy, not reflecting where ever it was AJ stood.

AJ blinked, startled.

Another young man took his place. He was African-American, with a picked-out afro, a large nose, and big, liquid brown eyes. He gave her a toothy grin and started unbuttoning the white shirt he wore before he, too, was pulled out of view by a noose.

What the heck was happening? What was she seeing?

Another young man took his place. Then another. Surprisingly, then came a young woman. All of them were amazingly good-looking. All of them were suggestive and flirtatious.

All of them were abruptly pulled out of view by a rope around their neck.

More people appeared and disappeared. AJ counted a solid dozen in all before the mirror itself started to back away, as if being pulled by an invisible hand. Then it turned to the side, the face of the mirror gone black.

AJ *was* standing in a loft. The house was an A-frame, with a loft on either end and an open floor plan below. The far loft was filled with some sort of smoke that gradually cleared.

Something was hanging from a beam in the loft on the other side of the house.

No.

Someone.

A body, with hair hanging down across the face. AJ couldn't tell if the person was male or female.

All she knew was that they were dead. This wasn't a symbol. When she saw a dead person in her vision, she knew she couldn't do anything to change the course of that person's path. When she was shown a symbol, she could help the person avoid their death, if she got to them in time. And if they'd listen to her. (Quite frankly, her score on that account wasn't great.)

Darkness abruptly filled the room. AJ gasped and came back to herself, sitting on hard (hot!) cement, with her sister's hand over her eyes.

"I'm okay," AJ said. Her voice came out ragged and her

head swam. She cleared her throat but that wasn't going to cut it.

"Here," Mom said, in that no-nonsense voice that all mothers acquired. "Get up. Come sit. Out of the sun."

Bea and Mom pulled AJ to her feet. She would admit to being slightly wobbly, but the sensation quickly passed as she took a few steps.

Mom pushed AJ down in her own lounge chair and handed her a bottle of water.

"Thanks," AJ said after taking a big swig of it. "I'm all right now," she insisted.

"Uh huh. You don't generally look this pale after a vision," Bea said, obviously not believing AJ.

"It...it was kind of a doozy," AJ admitted.

"What did you see?" Mom asked.

AJ sighed, then did her best to describe what had just happened.

Mom and Bea both gave her concerned looks.

"So what was that?" AJ asked. "Did I just see the death of a serial killer? The leader of a cult killing themselves and all their followers dying? What the heck?"

"All I know is that you started moaning there, at the end," Bea said. "That was why I put my hand over your eyes."

"Thank you," AJ said, nodding. When she used her scrying bowl, she always had stones in her hand. Her body automatically dropped a stone into the still water to break her out of a vision when it had run its course.

With a large body of water, like the pool, just a stone wouldn't have done the trick.

"I know you don't have visions often," Mom said, still looking worried, "but these seem dangerous. What would have happened if you'd been driving or something?"

"Well, first of all, I don't drive much. Second, I would have pulled off the road," AJ said. "I had time to do that."

Mom didn't look convinced but let it rest.

"So now what?" Bea asked.

AJ shrugged. "We wait. I couldn't save whoever it is, even if I knew who it was. Their fate is sealed, as it were."

Bea didn't look very satisfied with that answer. Neither did Mom.

However, AJ walked away from them and jumped back into the pool when they started asking too many questions.

This was supposed to be a vacation.

Right?

The next morning, AJ came out to the kitchen area to find both Bea and Mom glued to their phones.

She helped herself to a cup of coffee before sitting down beside them.

"I'm assuming that someone has turned up dead?" AJ asked softly.

"Yep," Bea said. "The Milltown app is full of speculation about it."

AJ nodded. While the Milltown app was very useful in terms of learning all the gossip going on around town, it also, at least in her opinion, sometimes turned ordinary, generally nice people into an unthinking mob.

"Who was it?" AJ asked after a moment. She focused on the lovely coffee in front of her (Mom had brought the really fancy stuff from Seattle) and getting it into her system rather than pulling out her own phone.

Vacation. Remember?

"The app says that the person wasn't a resident, just a tourist who'd rented a house for a couple of weeks," Bea said.

Mom nodded, then pushed her phone over to AJ, which showed the listing for the rental. It was an A-frame, and the pictures of the interior matched the vision AJ had had.

"Do we know anything about the victim?" AJ said after pushing the phone back to her mom.

"Yeah, actually. Quite a lot," Bea said. "Seems that James Teaford was kind of famous. Well, maybe more like infamous. And it explains your vision, too."

AJ waited while Bea continued to scroll along on her phone.

She sighed. Dang it! She didn't want to pick up her phone. Not yet. Not until she had to go back to work.

"And?" she finally prompted Bea.

"Oh! Sorry. He was a catfish, and had been exposed on this reality TV show, *Lyin' Cheatin' Stealin'* about a month ago," Bea said as if that explained everything.

"A what? A fisherman? Of catfish?" AJ asked.

Mom gave her an understanding smile. "I know. I had to go look it up too."

"A catfish is someone who pretends to be someone else on the internet," Bea said. "Generally for attention, though frequently for money. This James had a dozen different personas and had milked thousands of dollars out of his victims."

"So all the people I saw, who got jerked out of the mirror, were his personas? The people he was pretending to be?" AJ said. That made a strange sort of sense, if this James had put a lot of time and effort into those characters. Plus, other people had believed them to be real. A lot of other people, it sounded like.

"I think so," Bea said slowly. She showed her phone to AJ.

She was on the site for the TV show, and was looking at some of the pictures of the various personas of Jacques.

AJ gasped at one. Yes! That was the first person she'd seen in the mirror. And that was the second. She'd seen that one as well. Not all of the people she'd seen in the mirror were listed as James's personas. Plus there were a couple who were listed whom AJ hadn't seen.

"So that explains my vision," AJ said as she pushed the phone back to Bea. She took another drink of her coffee—the nectar of life, really—as she tried to pull her thoughts together. "Did he hang himself?"

"There aren't that many details about his death," Bea said, sounding frustrated. "I mean, he did leave a suicide note, which is mentioned on the app. But the police also opened up a tip line, which they only do when they think there's foul play, right?"

AJ snorted. "Yeah, but I don't think that tip line is going to do them any good. If this James has thousands of victims, the line is going to be flooded with people saying, 'Good riddance.'"

"That's not what the fandom is saying," Mom said.

"The what?" AJ said.

"The show has a large fandom, you know, people who identify as fans," Mom explained. "The LCS Gang is what they call themselves. There's even a hashtag."

Great. Her mom knew more about this stuff than AJ did. She suddenly felt old.

"What is the fandom saying?" Bea asked before AJ did.

"I haven't watched the episode yet—it's behind a paywall—but the consensus is that James was completely unrepentant about what he'd done. His basic response was that people shouldn't be so stupid. They should have known better than to give a stranger on the internet money."

"So this show exposes people who are catfishing?" AJ said.

"And people who are unfaithful, as well as people who have stolen money from others," Mom explained. "The LCS Gang debate how truthful someone is being. They also have quite a fascination for the two hosts, Leon and Moe. Seems that the hosts play up the 'unresolved sexual tension' between the pair of them, though they both maintain that they're just good friends. Oh, look! There's even fanfic."

AJ didn't even have to ask before Mom went on, explaining the term.

"Stories about a romance between the two hosts. Some of these seem to be friendly stories, bromance tales, rated PG. Huh. There are also pages of them that come with content warnings about the M/M sex."

AJ closed her eyes and shook her head. Nope. She didn't want to know about it. Not even in the least. Not enough brain bleach to clean out those sorts of things.

"Well, *I* know that James didn't commit suicide," AJ said. "I wouldn't have had a vision if he had."

Mom and Bea both looked up from their phones and stared grimly at AJ.

"Now, Mom, I know you don't want me to get involved in this sort of thing. But I have visions specifically because I'm *supposed* to get involved." AJ sighed and looked at Bea. "I'm going to need to go back to Milltown early. Find Fred Hanson, see if he knows anything."

"The owner of that grocery store?" Mom asked.

"Yeah. He used to be the biggest gossip in town. Then he actually started writing, instead of just talking about writing. He still knows more about what's happening in Milltown than most people. Plus, he probably can put me in touch with the owner of that rental property, might even be able to get them to talk with me."

Bea nodded. "I'll drive you into town," she said. "But then I'll come back out and spend the last night with you, Mom," she assured the other woman.

"Some girls' getaway," Mom groused. "I get tied up with business all day yesterday, and now you're leaving."

"I'll try to make it up to you later," AJ promised. "I should go pack."

Bea shook her head. "First, we go have breakfast. I'm not driving you anywhere until after I have something to eat."

AJ grinned at Bea. "You got it."

Dealing with murder on an empty stomach was always a bad idea.

Chapter Four

AJ finished unpacking her bag then hurried out the door of her gorgeous Craftsman house, up the short walk to Main Street, then down to the Storm Brew Café. She'd seen Fred sitting in the front window of the café when Bea had driven by before dropping her off. Fortunately, he was still there as she approached the shop, rapidly typing away on the laptop he'd recently purchased. He'd made the switch from writing everything out by hand then typing it up, to typing directly onto the computer. It had made him even more productive, and he was getting even more writing done.

There were an amazing number of people in the café, especially given that it was midweek in the off-season. Then again, the weather hadn't changed yet. Maybe people were just prolonging their vacations.

Or perhaps having their own version of a girls' getaway? Hopefully, a more successful one than hers had been.

Juli was behind the counter, which lifted AJ's spirits. It wasn't that the other baristas weren't good. Juli just happened to be the best.

After waiting in line for her coffee (no homemade granola and yogurt—breakfast with Mom and Bea had been so big AJ probably wasn't eating lunch), AJ took her coffee into the other room and sat down next to Fred.

He looked the same as always, his hairline still receding, clumps of dark brown hair fringing the edges of his pale skull, his mustache drooping over pouty lips. Fred had always been thin, but he looked more wiry now. Whenever he got stuck on a scene, he went and walked, and was now getting in ten thousand steps a day or more. His chubby cheeks had sunk in some, actually making him look more handsome, though not as debonair as he considered himself to be. As usual, he wore a casual T-shirt, jeans, and work boots that had never seen a lick of work.

AJ sat in comfortable silence as Fred typed away for a few minutes before looking up. He actually seemed startled to see her there, as if he'd been so involved with his writing that he hadn't known what was going on around him. Yet another change, and probably a good one.

"Ah! My muse! To what do I owe this delightful visit?" Fred said with a great grin.

"Did you see the news about the latest murder?" AJ asked.

"I did," Fred said, picking up his own long-forgotten coffee cup, taking a sip, and then making a face. It must have grown cold. "A catfish! How fascinating. I may have to put that in a story sometime."

AJ couldn't help but shake her head and roll her eyes. That tended to be Fred's response to just about everything these days.

"What do you know about the crime?" AJ asked.

She'd never figured out who Fred talked with, but he almost always knew more than anyone else about the goings-on in Milltown. He was always careful about his knowledge as well. He knew that it was valuable, and sold it at a high price sometimes.

Fred gave AJ a calculating look. "I'll tell you what I know if you tell me what you know."

AJ shrugged. "I don't know much, honestly."

"But you *saw* something?" Fred asked archly.

AJ nodded. Fred was one of the few people in town who knew she had actual visions.

"That will have to do, then," Fred said, nodding. "Okay. There was a suicide note. However, the police are fairly certain it wasn't suicide, that the scene was staged."

He waited, and AJ gave him the expected, "Go on."

"First of all, how did he get up there? To hang himself? There should be a chair or something that the person would have stepped up on, then off. The chair that was up there was a few feet from the victim, and still upright, not kicked over," Fred said.

"So maybe he jumped from the chair? To get a sharper yank on the rope?" AJ mused, playing devil's advocate.

"Possibly," Fred allowed. "But here's the real kicker. His hands were bound behind his back."

"Huh," AJ said. "So he couldn't stop himself?"

"That's one theory," Fred said, nodding. "However, the police don't think he could have tied himself up that way."

"The killer was really sloppy, then," AJ said. "Was it a crime of passion?"

"Probably not," Fred said. "That suicide note was written carefully. In it, James supposedly apologizes to all the people he harmed. Then he talks about all the hearts he broke, all the lives he ruined."

"But when he was on the show, he didn't have any remorse," AJ pointed out.

"Exactly," Fred said. "No one believes the note came from him. Plus, it was typed up and printed on a computer. However, there's no computer or printer in the rental house. The police are checking with the internet café down the street, and a couple of other places that offer people printing services, but that's just covering their bases. They're pretty sure that James didn't go into any of those shops."

AJ shook her head. "This just isn't adding up."

"I know that. The police know that. There aren't a lot of clues, though. The police can dust for prints, but it's a rental. There are hundreds of prints there."

A not very well cleaned rental. AJ was certain that the rooms in the Bridgewater Inn, where she worked part time, would have fewer leftovers from former guests. Rosita, who now owned the inn, took too much pride in thoroughly cleaning everything. Though now that AJ was thinking about it, probably not all the prints would be removed. Just most of them.

"There aren't any security cameras in that area either," Fred went on. "No one saw anything."

"Who found the body?" AJ asked.

"That's part of the problem," Fred admitted. "That reality TV show? *Lyin' Cheatin' Stealin'?* They're in town. Seemed someone called them and told them there was a follow up with Jacque. They told the show producers to meet with them at the rental unit. When the camera crew arrived, no one answered, and the door was wide open. They're the ones who found the body."

"Was it actually James who contacted them?"

Fred shrugged. "No idea. It was a voice message, but no

one actually talked to the company. However, the call did come from an online calling service that was only recently been activated, which is typically what catfishers use."

"Someone wanted that body found," AJ said.

"Probably the killer," Fred agreed.

But who was that?

AJ told Fred the details of her latest vision, cementing the notion that James really had been killed, that his death wasn't a suicide. She hadn't seen his face, as long hair had covered it, but she knew a dead body when she saw one. Even from a distance.

"So now what?" Fred asked.

"Do you know who owns the rental property?" AJ said. "And could you get me an introduction to them?"

Fred nodded. "I do. Kim Mayher. I'm sure she's right now overwhelmed with everything that's been going on, but I'll see if I can get her to talk with you later this afternoon."

"Thanks," AJ said. She didn't understand why she really needed to go and see the rental house, but she did.

As AJ was finishing up her coffee (and quite frankly considering getting more caffeine to go) a very handsome young man came up to her seat.

"Excuse me, are you AJ Steward?" he asked with a friendly smile. He wore what she'd consider work-casual clothes, a nice blue polo shirt, beige shorts, and loafers without socks. His hair was perfectly trimmed and probably dyed that shade of blond, and his intense blue eyes were the result of colored contacts.

AJ felt herself go on red alert instantly, all her instincts crying out, "Warning! Warning! Danger!"

"I am," she said slowly. "Who is asking?"

"I'm Leon Cooper, one of the hosts for the TV show *Lyin' Cheatin' Stealin'*. Have you heard of us?"

"I just read about you this morning," AJ said. "I'm sorry, but there isn't anything I can tell you about James."

"But you're a psychic, right? Surely you must know something," Leon said, his smile growing sharp.

AJ suddenly realized that there was a camera pointed at her, from the corner.

What the hell was going on? Were they going to try to make her part of the show? No one profiled by them ever turned out to be innocent.

AJ stood up slowly. "I don't know what game it is that you're trying to play, Mr. Cooper," AJ said. "But I do not give my consent to be on your show, or to be recorded. Is that clear?"

"Of course! Of course!" Leon said, backing away, his hands in the air.

AJ knew that it didn't look good, her refusing to talk with them. That they'd play that up as if it confirmed her guilt.

She shook her head and stalked out of the café, stepping into the sunshine.

Unfortunately, it didn't take away the chill she'd just received.

Chapter Five

Instead of going straight home, AJ started walking along the beach to clear her thoughts. The tide was coming in, and the waves rushed up to greet her. Terns ran beside her, poking their long beaks into any hole uncovered by the water. Gulls floated on the strong breeze, as if testing themselves, strengthening their wings for the upcoming stormy weather. The air smelled fresh and clean, waking her up more than the copious amounts of caffeine that she'd had that day.

Maybe she could go for a swim later. She did kind of have the day off. She'd gotten herself a wetsuit because the waters off the coast weren't ever warm, so swimming wasn't ever a spontaneous event. Plus, she always called her sister so she'd know where AJ was in case something happened to her out in the ocean.

Though water was AJ's element, that didn't mean she couldn't drown.

Probably.

What else could she do with an entire day off? Not seeing

clients or working at the inn? She did have that latest book to read…

She could already hear her sister warning that she better not go to the inn, to actually take some time for herself.

Feeling calmer, AJ turned around after reaching Sandy Point and started walking back.

It occurred to her that possibly all those people in the café had been part of the camera crew associated with the show. She'd watched half an episode while with her mom and Bea, and it seemed as though the hosts traveled with at least a dozen crew members.

It wasn't until she'd gotten close to the house that her phone rang. She looked at it suspiciously, but it was just Roland, her boyfriend.

"Hey there," she said warmly. "What's up?"

"Wanted to warn you that there's this reality TV show that's trying to get information about you," he said. "I just had to kick some people out of my office. You might want to extend your girls' getaway."

"Sorry they came to bother you," AJ said. "I'm already back from the getaway."

"Oh?" Roland said. "Everything okay with your mom?"

The warmth that AJ felt had nothing to do with the bright sunlight or being so close to the ocean.

"Yeah, Mom's fine. She was busy with some sort of business deal the first day, so we didn't see much of her. Then I had a vision," AJ admitted. AJ continued going along the beach, walking past her house as she talked with Roland, telling him about what she'd seen.

"What can I do to help?" Roland asked when she finished.

Again, that lovely warmth, knowing that she had this man in her corner, ready to support her.

"Keep telling the TV-show people that you don't want to talk with them, that you have nothing to say," AJ said. "That you don't give your permission to record you."

Roland gave a rough laugh. "They weren't expecting a gardener to go all legalese on them."

AJ snorted. Though Roland himself was a historian, he'd been raised by two lawyers who'd always been disappointed that he hadn't followed in their footsteps. He had had a fairly contentious relationship with them at the time. AJ had yet to meet them, though Roland had offered their services to her more than once.

Maybe at some point she and Roland would take that step. Roland had met AJ's mother, after all.

However, other things had to happen first. Possibly even declarations of love, which they'd both held back on so far.

AJ thought she might love Roland. She'd trusted him with all her secrets—not only that she had visions, but could also do water magic.

They were both still dealing with pain in their past, so they continued to take it slowly. Maybe once the rush of the season was over, and the town went back to being sleepy and small, they'd both be able to take a breath and focus more on each another.

"The people from the show probably took you for a small-town hick," AJ said. Roland usually dressed the part, particularly during the summer when he was working outside all the time: worn T-shirts, stained jeans, hands leathered and tough. He still kept his well-trimmed beard soft, his neck shaved, and his smile always warm and welcoming.

"They did course correct pretty quickly once they realized they couldn't trick me into giving them an interview about you," Roland said. "Just keep telling them that you do not give them your permission to be filmed."

"Got it," AJ said.

"So what are you doing this evening?" Roland said, his voice going deep and flirty.

"Oh, I don't know. I guess I kind of do have a night off, in the middle of the week," AJ teased. "Why? You got something in mind?"

"Maybe," Roland said.

They arranged to have a picnic dinner that evening. Roland would bring over fixings. AJ just had to supply the wine.

She hung up feeling better than she had been. Roland had a way of lifting her spirits.

They'd had a bit of a rough patch when he'd found out about her magic, but he'd been determined to accept it. He told her that he just needed to get over himself if he wanted to stay with her, so he'd worked hard on it.

AJ appreciated the sentiment.

She finally turned to head back to her lovely Craftsman house. It was on the beach. Not close enough to be flooded, not unless a tsunami hit. Then, most of the town would be gone and not much anyone could do about that.

The off-white of the exterior shone brightly in the sunlight, while the burnt sienna trim gave it a sophisticated look. At some point, she was going to have to replace the light gray shingles. For now, the roof was solid. So was the foundation, as she'd paid to have that repaired before she'd moved in.

She enjoyed how stately her house looked. Even the round tower that stood just to the right of the front door made a great sitting room for her clients while they waited for her.

It wasn't until she'd drawn close that she realized that there were people there.

Waiting for her.

Directing cameras toward her.

The people from that reality TV show weren't going to give her a moment's peace.

Chapter Six

A different man stood on AJ's front step, not the guy she'd met in the café. She recognized him from the stills she'd seen of the show: Moe Saxman, the other host.

He was taller than Leon by at least a couple inches. While Leon was blond and pretty, Moe struck her as dark and intense. He had deep-set eyes that looked nearly black as he stared at her. His dark hair hung artfully down over his forehead, giving him a bad boy air. He wore a brown T-shirt over black jeans, and slouched where he stood.

"I'm closed for the day," AJ told the man as she walked up the steps. "And I don't give you permission to record me," she added, looking out at the gathered half-dozen people all holding cameras pointed at her.

"Ah, don't be that way," Moe said in a wheedling tone that grated on AJ's nerves.

"I do not give my permission for you to record me," AJ said again, crossing her arms over her chest and staring at the camera crew.

One of the older men, with gray hair and a large rig that he wore on his shoulder stuck his head out from behind the eyepiece of his equipment. He took one long look at her, then nodded and lowered his gear.

The rest of the crew slowly followed suit.

AJ waited until they'd all turned away, walking out of her front yard and beyond the gate before she turned back to Moe.

"This is my home, as well as my place of business," AJ said frostily. "And you don't have an appointment. So I don't have to actually listen to you. But I'm giving you the chance to say something, now, quickly, before I kick you out."

Moe's eyes narrowed, then he nodded at her. "We know that you've helped the police in the past, though reports of that are kind of muddled," he started off with, ticking off one finger on his hand. "We know that James was murdered and his 'suicide' was staged. We suspect that you're already involved, given that you came back early from your vacation and met with Fred Hanson, the town gossip, first thing."

AJ's chill came back with a vengeance, a shiver running down her spine. "You're spying on me?" she said, shocked.

"No, no, we're not surveilling you," Moe said dismissively. "It's a small town. People talk. Particularly when they think they're going to be on camera. Plus, we have a large fanbase who are happy to send us tips."

AJ snorted. That, at least, was true. Milltown was a small town and people *did* talk.

Did the LCS Gang already have someone on the Milltown app? The owner of the app insisted that any person applying for membership have a local address. Logon credentials were mailed to the applicant, so it took a while before anyone was granted access.

However, if a local who was on the Milltown app was also

in the fandom...they could be supplying the crew with information.

"So why are you here?" AJ said. "What do you want from me?"

Moe crossed his arms over his chest and looked out at the ocean, away from AJ. Was he trying to make up his mind about what to say? Or was he just making sure that his crew was far enough away and that they were no longer recording?

"You haven't watched the show, I take it?" Moe asked.

"I watched half an episode yesterday, when the news came out about James's death, but that's about it," AJ admitted.

"Leon is the 'face' of the show. I'm the brains," Moe said. "Both on TV as well as in real life. The show's done well, but it's rare for this kind of product to have much longevity. We've had nine seasons, and there are rumors about cancellation."

AJ nodded. She got the sense that Moe was actually telling her the truth. She didn't understand why he was telling her this, but she did appreciate it.

"I want to be prepared to jump ship. To hit the network with a new viable product before we get any sort of notice about the show ending."

"One without your partner, I take it?" AJ asked.

"Exactly," Moe said. He turned his intense eyes toward her. "The show only airs episodes where people are actually guilty. We've started filming more than once, and then it turns out that the people weren't guilty of what they'd been accused of. Particularly because my stupid partner is convinced he's right, and he won't listen to the producers. However, it takes a lot more effort to prove guilt, which is part of why the network might not renew us. I'd rather have a show that takes a more nuanced approach, with episodes where it turns out people aren't fakes. That there is some good in the world."

AJ blinked, surprised. Moe seemed passionate about this—instead of just tearing people down, he wanted the opportunity to also lift people up.

"So where do I fit in?" AJ said.

Moe gave her an appraising look. "I think you're the real thing. I had people research you. No one has complained about your services. The local app gives you good ratings. You seem to care about people, and aren't just out to fleece them."

"What does your partner think?" AJ had to ask.

"He sees 'psychic' and assumes the worst," Moe said, rolling his eyes. "I've done interviews with real psychics, people who have powers that can't be explained. Now, I'm not naïve. I know that most of those people are fakes."

Moe paused, staring again at AJ. "My gut tells me you're the real deal. And I'd like you to help us get to the bottom of this."

AJ paused for a moment, then shrugged.

Gabby, a fire witch who'd been helping AJ with her magic, had tried to teach AJ *farsense*, the ability to see something occurring in real time, close by.

AJ had never mastered the skill. She speculated that it was partly because her visions were primarily of the future, not of the past or present.

However, AJ had a skill that Gabby didn't possess: the ability to tell when someone was lying.

Both of them could sense magic from another person when they were actively doing something magical. AJ's ability appeared to be stronger than Gabby's, even before she'd started working on it.

Not many people in the world had magic. An even smaller percentage could tap into their abilities.

AJ put a hand out toward Moe, closed her eyes, and tried

to sense what he was doing when he said his gut told him that she was the real thing.

Could she sense a type of magic coming from him? Or was it just a regular human intuition thing?

Moe gasped.

AJ opened her eyes.

"What—what were you just doing?" Moe said, his gaze now on her hand.

"Seeing if I could tell where your intuition was coming from," AJ said.

"Your hand started glowing," Moe said, his eyes rapidly shifting from AJ's hand to her face and back again. He wore an expression of disbelief, peering closely at her as if trying to figure out where the special effects were coming from.

"Huh," AJ said. "Never had that happen before." She wasn't going to think about it now. Maybe she'd have to do some experiments, maybe with Roland. She paused for a moment, then made a decision.

"I believe you," AJ said. "You're telling the truth. I can always tell when someone lies to me." That might have been a bit of a stretch, but it was close enough. "I will help you," she continued, then gave him a great grin. "Would you like to come in and have a reading?"

Chapter Seven

AJ pulled her tarot cards out of the black velvet bag she kept them in.

No matter what the temperature of the room the card bag was in, the cards themselves always felt warm to the touch. Not hot chocolate warm, more like fuzzy, comfortable blanket warm.

Moe sat across the sturdy oak table from her in her reading room. The soothing blue-green walls always calmed her, and the sconces she'd added when she'd redecorated looked like seashells. A "crystal" ball of white, cloudy selenite sat on the table between her and her client. She'd gotten that at the insistence of Willow, one of the people she worked with at the Bridgewater Inn. Willow might have a type of magic, earth magic, but it was so weak she'd never been able to do anything with it.

The selenite was supposed to provide purity and cleansing of the room. AJ had never gotten any feeling from it beyond a sense of satisfaction.

Moe eyed the crystal suspiciously, but didn't said anything.

He appeared much more interested in her scrying bowl and the crystal water pitcher that sat beside it.

But AJ wasn't there to have a vision—the water in the pitcher wasn't glowing and she didn't feel any urge. The cards, though, felt right in her hands.

"We'll start off doing a three-card draw for you, Moe," AJ said as she smoothly shuffled the cards.

Moe sat back in his chair, leaning away from her. "Why," he asked flatly.

"To get a reading on where you are in all this," AJ said. "A three-card draw is the quickest thing we can do. First card is past, middle card is present, and the third card is future. Got it?"

"Sure," Moe said.

AJ handed him the cards. "Shuffle please."

Moe looked a little confused, but did as he was asked, shuffling them with the expertise of a Las Vegas poker dealer.

AJ watched closely. He was actually mixing the cards together, and not trying to stack the deck, though she suspected he'd thought about it. Then again, she wasn't sure how familiar he was with a tarot card deck, and if he'd know how to arrange the cards to be favorable for him.

Plus, she had her own interpretation of most of the suits, so even if he did try to stack the cards, the reading might still be significantly different than someone who only looked at the traditional meanings.

Once he finished, she had him place the deck between them.

"Cut them," she said.

He picked up the top two thirds of the deck, putting it on the table, then adding the remaining third of the cards to the top of the deck.

"Draw the first card horizontally, not vertically," AJ instructed. "So the orientation remains the same as the deck."

Moe nodded and did as she requested.

AJ snorted as the first card was revealed.

The Lovers, reversed.

"Hmmm. A relationship," she said dryly.

Moe rolled his eyes and shook his head, then turned his intense stare at her. "You couldn't have stacked the cards for that to come up first. I was the only one to touch the deck at the end."

"I know," AJ said softly.

Moe pressed his lips together before he gestured for her to continue.

"The Lovers represents relationships. This time, however, it's also reversed, which can represent the fall of a relationship," AJ said. "Also, plans that have gone awry, innocence taken."

When had Moe and Leon's falling out occurred? It hadn't happened recently. Moe had been planning on leaving for a while, AJ would bet.

"Next card, please."

Moe nodded and flipped over the following card.

It was the six of swords, not reversed. A man stood at the back of a boat, using a pole to move it across a body of water. To his left the surface of the water was smooth and clear, while on the right, it was choppy. His passengers were a cloaked figure with a child. Six swords stood around the front of the boat, almost like a cage.

"Journeys, generally," AJ said. "A card of movement, of not being settled. Possibly of being trapped by always moving, never able to reach the shore due to the swords. This is the present. Moving yet stagnant. Stuck despite the change of scenery."

Moe gulped but didn't say anything.

AJ indicated that he should turn over the last card.

"The knight of cups, upright," AJ said. "Another figure of movement. Notice the wings on his helmet and his boot. He carries news—possibly also visions and dreams—as he moves forward. His armor is decorated with fish, the reins of the horse have waves on them, and he is approaching a river."

Moe peered curiously at the card. Maybe no one had pointed out all the details to him before.

"Like the six of swords, the knight of cups is a card of journeys. But instead of being ferried, the knight is directing his own path. He's something of a dreamer—that's something all the in the suit of cups have in common. But he's more purposeful now. Moving forward to his own tempo, following his own path."

AJ sat back and let Moe ponder what she'd just said. "That was real, wasn't it?" he said after a few moments.

AJ shrugged. "As real as this sort of thing can be, finding meaning in random symbols."

"Is this really psychic work?" Moe asked.

"You want me to tell you my theory?" AJ said with a grin.

"Sure."

"Symbols tap into our brains in a different place than words. Deeper. So even if the words aren't necessarily what you need to hear—aren't the correct psychic part—the symbols are. They'll unlock the subconscious and open up possibilities that words can't," AJ said.

Moe nodded. "So are you a fake?"

AJ continued to grin at him. "What do you think?"

"I still think you're the real deal," he said slowly. "I'm not sure what this all was, if I believe this. It wasn't magic."

AJ blinked but neither confirmed nor denied what he'd just said. She honestly wasn't sure.

"What I think you're telling me, though, is that I can make it on my own, finding my own path, away from the relationship that's currently soured," Moe said.

"I think so. I'd probably think that, though, even without the cards. You seem pretty driven," AJ said honestly.

Moe gave her a brief smile. "So I'm told."

"Pick up the cards and shuffle them when you're finished looking at them," AJ told Moe.

After a few more moments, he did that with a nod, shuffling the deck precisely then handing it back to her.

"Now what?" he asked her.

AJ nodded. "I'm waiting for Fred Hanson to get back to me with an invite to talk with Kim Mayher, to go and look at the rental."

"The owner of the rental?" Moe said. "Why do you want to go there?"

AJ shrugged. "I'm not sure. I just know that it's important, that I see the site where James was killed." It was an odd urge for her, but she couldn't deny it.

Moe thought for a moment, before he nodded. "Did you know that Kim Mayher is part of the LCS gang?"

"I did not," AJ said surprised.

"She was pretty excited to hear that we were coming to town," Moe said. "And more than happy to let us film in the vacation rental."

"Was she the one who tipped you off that he was staying at that vacation rental?" AJ asked.

Moe grimaced. "She denies that she did, but I'm not sure I believe her. Leon believes her, of course."

"All right—can you get us an interview with her?" AJ said, automatically including Moe in on the visit.

"Already have one for five PM today," Moe told her with a grin.

"Great," AJ said. "Should I meet you there?"

Moe nodded. "You may have to rescind your statement about not being filmed. I need to show up with a crew for Kim to be happy."

"How about just you, me, and a portable camera, so you can take some stills?" AJ suggested as a compromise. "Would that be enough for her? I'm sure she's already been interviewed by your people."

After a moment's consideration, Moe nodded. "I can do that."

They exchanged contact information and said their good-byes. AJ glanced at the time. It was close to two. She had a few hours.

She could hear Bea telling her to *not* go into the inn and do any work today. She had the day off. She should take it.

AJ went into her cozy kitchen and poured herself a glass of lemonade. Then she walked out the door into her backyard. A tall wooden fence, painted white, enclosed the small area, high enough that no one could see over it. Bea kept threatening to come over and decorate it someday. So far, AJ had managed to hold her off. But she wouldn't be surprised if she came home one night and found an explosion of color across her fence.

Roland had built planter boxes around the edges of the space. Because the weather had remained nice, they were still filled with flowers, including purple and red petunias, bright pink pansies, white bellflowers, and yellow marigolds. One held herbs, like chocolate mint for her tea, basil, thyme, rosemary, and oregano. AJ wasn't the best with plants—they required a lot more maintenance than she was comfortable with. Still, she'd managed to keep everything alive all summer long. Roland had told her that all the plants would die back come fall, but most of them could come back in the spring. He was planning on bringing her some mums once the weather turned cooler.

A fountain gaily burbled in the center of the space. While the base of it was made from white painted concrete, about three feet across, the center was made from patinaed brass. It stood about three feet tall, with shapes of fruits and vines cascading down its sides.

The sound of the water always relaxed AJ, as did her ocean view. Water was her element. While she'd done some experiments with water before she'd met Gabby, she'd become more systematic about it since their encounter.

AJ picked up a comfortable cushion from a box next to the backdoor, then put it on the stones that surrounded the fountain, leaning against the warm concrete and dipping her hand into the cool water.

In the past, AJ had used water as a shield, to protect herself. However, she'd been standing in a heavy rain at the time, and the water all around her had bent to her will.

She was starting to play with the possibility of some sort of armor formed by water.

As she lifted her hand from the fountain, she focused on spreading the water out, coating her hand, then thickening it, until it encased her skin like a glowing, translucent blue glove. While she could extend the coverage to just past her wrist, once the water encountered mostly dry skin, it wouldn't go farther.

Try as she might, just a trickle of water going from her shoulder down her arm wasn't enough to get the armor to encase more. Water went where it had already been. It didn't like going places where it hadn't been, and the small amount of water she'd added wasn't enough. Her arm had to be mostly wet for the watery armor to climb up further.

AJ had been dealing with this for weeks now. How could she get the water to protect her when she wasn't soaking wet?

Bea had suggested that AJ start working with a water gun, leaning more on offense than defense. AJ had quickly learned that a kid's water gun didn't deliver enough volume of water to be effective. She needed a super sprayer to do any damage.

Instead, AJ had started carrying a large-mouthed water bottle everywhere she went. Throwing that amount of water into the air gave her enough liquid to work with. She'd gotten a lot faster turning the thrown water into a meaty punch that landed where she directed it. Even if she threw the water in front of her, she could still make the water turn and punch behind her.

So AJ spent time that afternoon trying to determine the minimum amount of water necessary for protection, or if she was just going to have to dump her entire water bottle over her head. The latter seemed to give her the best results.

Fortunately, AJ was already adept at drying herself off after being soaked. Winter on the coast, in the Pacific Northwest, had certainly honed that skill.

Hopefully, she was overthinking this whole thing, and she wouldn't need this level of protection.

Better to be safe than sorry, though.

Chapter Eight

The locals from Milltown often joked that the town was two blocks wide and two miles long. That wasn't really the case. While most of the town's shops were along Main Street, which ran north-south and parallel to the shoreline, people's homes were up in the hills that over looked the commercial district. The neighborhoods went on for a good ways, making Milltown more than just two blocks wide.

AJ had plenty of opportunities to walk up those steep hills, as her sister Bea lived a few blocks up off Main Street, back in one of the more eclectic neighborhoods. Her mother's new vacation rental was in the same general vicinity, though a few more blocks to the north.

To get to the A-frame rental where James had been killed, AJ took the street that peeled off Main Street going up the hill toward her sister's place. However, the rental was a few more blocks east, further up the hill. AJ paused and took some deep breaths when she was about halfway there, regretting her decision to walk. Still, when she turned around, the view of the ocean was lovely. Not as good as from the front of her house, but good enough. Maybe. If you didn't have anything better.

The street leading toward the rental was wide and paved at first, with no sidewalks, of course. (The only sidewalks in all of Milltown were along Main Street. That was it. Locals joked about how the town might perhaps someday join the 1950s.)

The paved street ended in what looked like a cul-de-sac. However, at the end of it, a dirt road continued, with large signs at the edges of it proclaiming it to be private property, a private road, as well as a dead-end.

AJ stepped off the pavement into the trees, the warm September air instantly cooling. It smelled green back there, with baked pines and sweet mulch. Dust still hovered a few inches above the road, probably from cars that had recently passed.

The second house from the end was the A-frame. While the front of it looked out on the dirt road, she'd seen pictures on the vacation rental site that showed that the back of the house looked out on trees. A Jeep with a bright pink sticker across the back, proclaiming that Jeeps were a girl's thing, was parked to one side. A nondescript black rental car, with California plates, sat beside it.

Moe stood by the front door talking with a small Asian woman. Even given the heat of the day, she wore a long-sleeved T-shirt done in baby blue with white flowers on it, what looked like heavy jeans, and solid hiking boots. Black fingerless gloves covered her hands, with copper-colored dots along the backs of them, situated on her knuckles and encircling her wrists. Her only concession to the heat was that her long black hair was up in a messy bun, with two chopsticks artistically stabbing it.

"Hey, AJ, glad you could meet us here," Moe said as she walked closer. "This is Kim Mayher. Kim, this is my friend AJ, who's here to help me with the photographs." He handed off a small camera to her.

AJ recognized that Moe's voice as not quite real. However, he wasn't trying to schmooze her, but rather Kim.

"Pleased to meet you," Kim said, nodding her head and not sounding pleased in the least.

AJ noticed the yellow police caution tape done in an X over the front door. "Can we go in?" she asked.

Kim huffed. "We can go in the back door. Just don't move anything. That's really what the police ask. I still can't believe that they won't release the house back to me! I have customers this weekend!"

The shrillness of Kim's voice set AJ's back up. She still maintained a pleasant demeanor. "I'm sure that the officers will release it soon," she said soothingly. She wondered if Officer Brendan was the one responsible for the hold, or if it was Officer Naomi. Had Kim managed to rankle them?

"They better," Kim muttered. Then she seemed to remember herself. "I'm sure that since you and your team are here, they'll release it soon. Particularly if you ask for them to."

AJ kept smiling and didn't roll her eyes at the blatant attempt at manipulation.

"I'll see what I can do," Moe said.

AJ nearly snorted. That was a complete lie. He had no intention of intervening with the cops.

"In the meanwhile, can we take a look around?" Moe asked. "Get some still shots for the show?"

"Of course!" Kim said, practically simpering. "You know, when I bought this place five years ago, I never imagined that I would ever have such prestigious guests!"

She led them down a narrow walkway next to the house. The house was longer than AJ had expected, maybe fifty feet.

The roof of the A-frame jutted out, keeping the walkway dry and shaded. Trees filled the area just a few feet away.

AJ glanced in through the windows curiously. They passed by the kitchen and what looked like a bedroom on the way back.

"All the walls on the ground floor are movable," Kim was saying when AJ tuned back into the conversation. "Like shoji, from a Japanese house. That way guests can configure the space to their needs. Either a completely open floorplan, or with one or two bedrooms. Plus additional sleeping space in the two lofts."

"Clever," Moe said, sounding earnest for once.

The back of the house was like the front, the first floor covered in windows with a small amount of dark-red painted wood between the huge pieces of glass. A small patio extended into the trees back here, but there wasn't much of a view past the greenery.

No ocean view either, which made AJ knock her appraisal down quite a few notches. It was quiet though, and pretty enough. If you liked trees.

Kim unlocked the door and invited them in. A musty house scent wafted out at them, which made AJ feel relieved.

She'd been really afraid that the house would smell like blood. Or worse.

At Moe's gesture, AJ walked in first. She realized that this was close to the location from where she'd had her vision. She looked up. Yes, there was a flat ceiling above her head instead of the peaked roof, that was probably the floor of the loft.

It was a big space, about twenty feet across, mostly open, as the moveable walls were all pushed to one end at this point.

At the far side, AJ could see the second loft. That was where James had been found.

AJ wasn't interested in going there. Instead, she immediately walked to the ladder for the closest loft and started going up it.

Ugh. She'd hate living someplace like this. Just imagine needing to get up in the middle of the night to go to the bathroom, and having to negotiate such a steep ladder!

The loft was mostly empty. Closet rods were strung along both walls, providing extra space for clothes. Two small windows at the far end brought in what little light that could escape through the looming trees.

Something dark stood against the wall to her right. It wasn't until AJ was practically on top of it that she realized it was a cheval mirror. The surface was pushed toward the wall, so she couldn't see herself in it.

"What's this?" AJ said as she reached for the mirror.

"I'd forgotten that was up here," Kim lied badly.

Huh. Why had she lied about that?

AJ swung the mirror around.

For a moment, the surface of the mirror appeared gray and dull before it transformed and became reflective.

AJ stepped to the side and carefully photographed it with the camera that Moe had handed her. Moe did the same with his camera.

"It's a beautiful piece," AJ told Kim as she carefully replaced the mirror exactly as she'd found it.

"Thank you," Kim said. "It's been in the family for awhile."

That was...true. Kim did like the mirror. AJ had the feeling that the woman had hauled it up that ladder some time ago, hiding it here in this loft. But why?

AJ took pictures of the far loft from where she was standing. There wasn't anything in the other loft. The noose had been taken down. No body hung there. She still shivered, looking at it. It didn't seem real.

"AJ?" she finally heard Moe say.

"Ah, yeah?" she said in response, blinking.

"You okay? You seemed really zoned out there for a bit," he said. He actually sounded worried about her.

"I'm fine," AJ said. She shook her head and looked around.

Kim looked at her curiously. "I know you," she said slowly. "You live here. You're the psychic!"

AJ smiled at her. "Guilty as charged."

"Are you actually working with her?" Kim said, shooting a glare at Moe.

"Of course, I'm *working* with her," Moe said.

AJ kept her snort to herself. Reading between the lines, it was easy to see that Kim thought Moe was setting AJ up for a fall, to be exposed on the *Lyin' Cheatin' Stealin'* show.

She didn't think he was, though she was aware that she needed to be careful around him.

After going back down the ladder, Kim led them through the rental, giving them a sales pitch about its charms and appeal.

AJ would never rent such a place. Though it had a lot of square footage, it still only had one bathroom. If she needed to put someone up, she'd use the inn. Still, it was nice to hear about someone else's setup, how visitors could cook for themselves in the kitchen, and Kim would bring in extra cots and blowup beds as required.

None of them walked up the ladder to the other loft. Even Moe didn't want to get any closer to it.

After the tour, and after AJ had taken many photos that she was sure were useless, they walked back out the back door.

AJ accepted Moe's offer of a drive into town after they'd said their goodbyes to Kim.

"So, whatcha think?" Moe asked as they started down the dirt road.

"She's hiding something," AJ said immediately. "First of all, she'd put that mirror up there for a reason. And she's lying about other things."

"Like what?"

"I don't know. Maybe your people can find out," AJ said.

Moe nodded. "I'll look into it. We haven't found anything hinky about her yet, though."

"Okay," AJ said. "Thanks."

"What's next?" Moe asked.

"Tonight's the chamber of commerce meeting, and I need to attend that," AJ admitted. "Then I might try to see if I can have another vision."

"Good. Let me know," Moe said. He paused, then added, "What happened to you, standing in the loft? You really seemed to space out for awhile."

AJ shrugged. "Don't know. Not something I normally do. But there's something about that place, something with that mirror, and Kim."

They drove in silence back down to Main Street, and Moe dropped AJ off at the inn.

She stood in the circular driveway, a cold wind blowing in from the ocean.

The oh-so-nice weather was going to turn. Soon.

AJ felt as though she was running out of time.

For what? Summer? To solve this mystery? She didn't know.

But she didn't like it.

Chapter Nine

Just past the elevators in the inn was a broad staircase that led to the second and third floors. While most of the floors were taken up with rooms, the third floor held some awkward conference rooms.

There'd been much debate between Rosita and her sisters about what to do with those spaces. They'd originally all been one big room. Someone in the seventies had put in walls, dividing the space up. The original center of the large area remained intact, with its huge fireplace and original blue-green tile mantle. The other rooms had conference tables and chairs. However, only a few groups rented the spaces—like the writer's group that came annually and used all the conference rooms as writing rooms during the week they rented the entire place.

The chamber of commerce didn't have its own building, but instead, met at the various venues in town that could cater to the large group. This month it was AJ's turn, and so the meeting was being held at the inn.

As she was a bit early, AJ checked on the conference room, making sure it was set up. Of course, Rosita, or more likely one of her sisters, had everything ready, including urns with both decaf and regular coffee, hot water with tea bags, and four dozen cookies baked by Payne Thomas, the chef who worked at the inn. The table in the center of the space held pitchers of cold water and glasses.

AJ grabbed herself a cookie and some decaf then made herself comfortable at the table.

Lionel was the next to arrive. He gave her a big, "Hello there!" when he saw her. He wore an impeccably stylish outfit, as always, this time a fitted tan polo that showed off his muscular black forearms, khaki pants that looked casual but AJ would bet were anything but, and brown loafers. No hat this time, and his black hair had been shaved close to his scalp.

"Ah, Payne must have known I was coming," Lionel commented as he looked at the cookies. "I see chocolate chip, chocolate chunk with marshmallow and walnuts, and a peanut-toffee crunch cookie."

"Was he fixing all of those just for you?" AJ asked, smiling when the big man took one of each cookie. She hadn't looked at the cookies closely enough to identify each. Now, looking down, she realized she'd unconsciously grabbed the chocolate chunk.

Of course she had. Even without registering it, she'd picked the cookie with the biggest pieces of chocolate in it.

Lionel sighed slightly as he sat down, studying the cookies in front of him. "He's tried my chocolate chip cookies, and has been urging me to do some experiments with them. But I love my recipe! It's always successful." He took a bite from the chocolate chunk cookie. "However, this is exceptional."

AJ nodded and took another bite of her own. The chunks of chocolate were perfect, not too bitter, not too sweet. The marshmallow gave it a gooey texture when she bit into one of those pieces. And she loved the nuts, the crunch factor, as well.

Payne could bake cookies well, as long as he stuck with the more traditional recipes. Other dishes were more miss than hit. Sometimes AJ despaired of his endless need to experiment. She wouldn't have minded it so much if he actually had an adequate palate.

"So what's new on your end of town?" AJ asked Lionel when he finally finished tasting (and judging) each of the different types of cookies.

"Business has been good," Lionel said. "The nice weather has helped. At least this year."

Lionel owned many different properties in Milltown, including both business buildings and vacation rentals. He felt he still needed to perfect his recipes before starting up his own baked good shop. AJ had tried his cinnamon rolls and thought that just on the basis of those he could go into business. It was always a delight when Lionel hosted the chamber of commerce meetings, as the treats he provided were amazing.

AJ did a double take when her mom walked in the door next.

"Mom? What are you doing here? Are you okay? Is Bea okay?" AJ asked, hurriedly standing and rushing over to her mom's side.

"Everything's fine, dear," Irene Steward assured her as she leisurely walked over to the table holding the coffee and treats.

AJ stood there, blinking in confusion, as her mom helped herself to a cup of decaf and one of the peanut-toffee crunch cookies. (Her mom wasn't that into chocolate. Weirdo.)

"Ah, Mom? You know that this is the chamber of commerce meeting, right? It's only for people who have a business in Milltown?"

Dread filled AJ as the words left her mouth.

"I know, dear," her mom said as she put her cookie and drink down on the table next to AJ's. "Hi, I don't believe we've met. My name is Irene Steward. I recently purchased the interior decorating business known as Design Solutions," she continued, holding out her hand to Lionel while throwing a smirk at AJ.

"Nice to meet you," Lionel said, shaking her hand.

AJ continued to gape.

"What?" she finally came out with. "You own a business in Milltown? Since when?"

"Last week," Mom said airily. The smile she gave AJ had something of an evil tint to it.

And her statement wasn't quite the truth.

AJ narrowed her eyes. "No. Really. Since when?"

Mom gave a large, put upon sigh. "Fine. The paperwork hasn't been finalized yet. But that's just a matter of a few signatures. All the negotiations are done, as of Tuesday morning." Her mom gave AJ a defiant look. "That was the meeting I was taking."

AJ realized that her mother had been on the phone a lot that morning, while they were supposedly on a girls' getaway. She opened her mouth to ask why, but then closed it again.

She knew why.

Her mom always had to meddle. Always. She'd probably been researching companies she could purchase for months, even before she'd come down that spring to visit her daughters for the first time.

"We're going to talk about this later," AJ said archly as she sat back down.

Fortunately for her, before her mom could start pestering her about what they needed to talk about, a large influx of people arrived and AJ was introducing Irene when she wasn't introducing herself.

Nothing good was going to come of her mother's involvement in the town's chamber of commerce.

AJ didn't have to be a psychic to know that.

———

Sandy Gerlach was the current president of the chamber of commerce. AJ always enjoyed her no-nonsense approach. She ran Sandy's Grill, a restaurant at the other end of town.

The difference between Sandy and her mom was striking. Sandy dressed in a loose oatmeal-colored pullover and khaki shorts, her whitish-blonde hair fizzy and untamed, while Irene wore a business chic outfit, peach-colored silk blouse and a dark-blue pencil skirt. Sandy had meaty hands that she used to bang on the conference table to bring everyone to order, her skin reddened by the sun and the wind. Irene had just had her nails done in a French manicure and her makeup was impeccable.

Still, Irene gave Sandy the proper respect as she was introduced, and seemed content to just listen during the recitation of old business, which included talk of the Halloween event the town held annually, the Turkey Trot race that they'd participate in with their neighboring towns, and the start of the Christmas/holiday celebrations.

When the time for new business came around, Irene introduced herself again, letting everyone know that she was now a business owner in Milltown and was looking forward to working with all of them. She did ask about the next Milltown Open, if there would be a BBQ competition the following year.

Fortunately, Sandy was able to reply to that, stating that the negotiations with the Left Coast Barbecue Association (LCBA) had already begun.

"I really enjoyed attending that event last year," Irene said with a large smile that AJ could tell was mostly genuine.

"Good," Sandy said in her brusque way. "I can sign you up for the committee then?"

AJ kept her smile to herself as her mom appeared a little taken aback at that.

"Sure," Irene said after a beat. "I'd be happy to help."

Had Sandy just made a mistake? Was this how Irene was planning on taking over the chamber of commerce?

Because AJ knew her mom, and her schemes. Probably nothing short of running the place would probably be good enough for her.

The meeting drew to a close. AJ looked over at her mom then said, "Why don't you come to my house for a nightcap?"

"I'd love to," her mom said with a tight smile.

AJ understood that her mother wasn't necessarily looking forward to divulging more of her plans to her elder daughter.

Too bad.

She shouldn't have made those plans in the first place if she wasn't planning on muscling into AJ's territory.

***

"So, Mom, why an interior design business?" AJ asked after she'd poured both of them a large glass of a good merlot back in the cozy kitchen of her house.

AJ had upgraded the appliances when she'd moved in, as well as laid down new linoleum that was white with a confetti pattern of pastel blues and greens. She'd repainted the cabinets white and the walls a sage green. She'd also put in a larger, farmhouse sink so she could easily stick her entire head under the water when she felt the need.

Like now, though she couldn't, not with her mom there.

"I've always been interested in decorating, dear," Mom said as she made her way to the tiny table that AJ had kept from the previous owner, (her mentor, Ursula) as it fit perfectly under the window looking out on the back yard.

AJ considered that for a moment before nodding her head. "True," she said. She stayed where she was, standing and leaning her hip against the far counter. Her mom hadn't had an annual redecoration budget for the house—unlike some of her friends. Still, AJ could remember there were always design magazines on the coffee table in the living room, and not just for show, as her mom generally read them cover to cover.

"Why now?" AJ asked, wondering what story her mother would try to tell her.

"I'm shifting more of my life down here, to Milltown," Mom said. "I may end up retiring here."

AJ didn't bother holding back her snort. It wasn't as if her mom actually had a job. She'd made enough from her divorce settlement with their long-absent father that she'd never have to work again. Instead, she volunteered as a member of the board of directors for various charities. She never did any of the actual volunteer work herself, such as working a food line at a food bank—no, she always managed the money end of things.

"What?" Mom asked, looking affronted.

"Please," AJ said. "I work, and will possibly retire someday."

"You girls never understood all that I did for my charities," Mom said, her voice surprisingly bitter.

AJ shrugged. That was true enough. It was also equally true that her mom had never worked a nine-to-five.

"What you saw was a lot of entertaining, me going to parties and attending events. You don't realize those were actually work, getting people with more money than sense to give me some of it," Mom continued.

AJ opened her mouth, closed it again, then took a swig of wine.

She was never going to convince her mother that talking people out of money wasn't actually work.

"So now, I'm going to put those same skills to the test and build up a business down here in Milltown," Mom continued. "I am certain I can do it, that I can turn this business around and that we'll be able to show a profit quickly."

"Okay," AJ said, a little surprised at her mom's passion. "You said design firm. What does that mean, exactly?"

"There are two parts to Design Solutions," Mom said with a firm nod, suddenly turning serious. "The commercial side and the consumer side. The commercial side is much larger, as they've had luck with some of the bigger building projects that have been taking place here on the coast. You know that new condo complex that went in just up 101? It's situated between Milltown and Sunset. Design Solutions did much of the interior work on those."

"I know the place you're talking about," AJ said as she walked over to where her mom was sitting and taking the other chair. She grimaced. "We had some issues with the developers at the start, as they were asking for a bunch of variances and didn't want to give anything in recompense."

"Really?" Mom said. "Danny did that?"

"Danny *tried* to do that." She knew exactly who her mom was talking about. Danny Schwartz owned the development company that had spearheaded those condos. They wanted variances in terms of the number of parking spots, in the amount of greenery around the buildings, even in their water systems.

The business owners of both Milltown and Sunset had come together to put the kibosh on the project. Though it had taken a lot of negotiations, eventually the towns and the development company had come to an agreement, with Danny and his crew getting very little of their original ask.

While the extra taxes and business from all those people moving in was a good incentive, the precedent it would have set would have been catastrophic.

After AJ explained all the background to her mom, she merely nodded. "You can't blame the man for trying," she said.

"Yes, Mom, I can," AJ said. "He was trying to strong-arm a little community like Milltown into giving him a lot for his project, including reduced taxes, and getting absolutely nothing in return."

Mom took a sip of her wine, considered for a moment, then looked up at AJ and gave her a blinding grin. "I've taught you well, haven't I?"

AJ scrunched up her face, confused. "How?"

"You read the contracts, all the way through," Mom said triumphantly.

"Of course we read the contracts," AJ said. "Though those variances were hard to miss." She paused, then added, "But yeah. You taught me to always redline the contracts before agreeing to anything."

Mom raised her glass in a silent toast.

"So are you only taking over the company so you'll have something to do?" AJ said, getting back on track as to why she was talking (and drinking) with her mom so late that night.

"Partly," Mom admitted. "But it's also partly the challenge. I've done charity work for so long. And while I prided myself on being able to bring in the most dollars for whatever cause I was working on, it was, in some ways, always a team effort. This? I'm doing this on my own. No real safety net. If I fail, it's my money on the line."

AJ blinked, surprised. She'd never thought if it that way.

"And the Milltown chamber of commerce?"

Mom grinned at her. "A way of getting to spend more time with my daughters!"

AJ could tell that was true enough.

However, there was still more, additional plots layered underneath.

AJ wasn't going to get to the bottom of this mystery tonight, though. She said goodbye to her mother soon afterward, and headed to her reading room, still considering all that she'd learned, all that she knew, while at the same time, trying not to fear what was to come.

Chapter Ten

AJ sat in her reading room, her scrying bowl filled with clear water, her head pounding.

Nothing was coming through in the way of a vision.

Nada.

AJ knew better than trying to force having a vision. And she hadn't been. Really.

Her current headache begged to differ with her.

Unsatisfied, AJ dragged herself upstairs to her bed, snagging a cold beanbag pillow that she kept in the freezer to take with her.

In the morning, AJ's headache had vanished.

So had the nice weather.

Clouds scuttled across the sky, chasing each other and playing tag, as if challenging themselves to see who could provide the darkest, gloomiest day. Cold winds whipped around AJ as she stepped from her house, nipping at any exposed skin and trying to find a way inside her warm jacket. It should be a light day at the inn, thankfully, and AJ would take the time to catch up on paperwork and inventory.

She stopped at the Storm Brew Café on her way into work, picking up a Juli "whatever" drink. AJ would hand Juli money and Juli would make for AJ whatever concoction she'd recently invented. Most of the time it was brilliant and just what AJ needed.

Though AJ was certain Juli didn't have any actual magic, sometimes her coffee drinks were so on point they seemed that way.

That morning, AJ had a dirty chai latte with peppermint that seemed to pick her right up as she made her way to the inn.

Willow worked the front desk, her demeanor slightly surly as always. AJ knew that Willow was actually caring and delightful, and she'd certainly put on a smile when a customer came in. Otherwise, she looked and acted more like an emo teenager, despite being twenty-three. Today she wore her usual over-sized man's shirt with a black vest, at least a half-dozen different stones on leather bands around her neck, and a gold nose ring.

AJ waved at Willow as she continued back to her office. Willow would call her if a line of guests formed, all wanting to either check in or out at the same time. Willow nodded at her but didn't say anything, just returned to whatever she was reading on the desk.

The office AJ had inherited from the original owners of the inn hadn't gone through that many changes. Instead of two desks there was now one, pushed against the wall that had a windows looking out on the back garden of the inn. AJ had taken down a lot of the pictures that had originally hung there, though she'd been slowly adding more back, including a piece of her sister Bea's artwork.

She'd finally replaced the old soup bowl that she'd borrowed from the inn's kitchen for a scrying bowl. Now, a pretty cut-glass bowl adorned one of the shelves behind her, so it never collected debris. She didn't want to have to empty it out if she was about to have a vision. She also had a small bowl full of binder clips that she used to break herself out of a vision if necessary.

AJ was a couple hours into her paperwork. She'd reached the point where she was considering taking a break, stretching her legs and wandering out to the dining area to help herself to some fresh coffee. Before she could get up, a knock sounded on her door.

"Come in!" AJ said leaning back and stretching slightly.

Willow poked her head in. "There's someone here to see you."

Moe stood behind Willow.

"Sure, send him in," AJ said, beckoning Moe into her office.

He looked around the office as he sat down, taking in the various pictures and the fairly clean state of her desk.

"What can I do for you?" AJ asked.

"I have a question about the pictures you took yesterday. A couple in particular," Moe said. He drew a tablet out of the bag he carried, turned it on, then slid it across her desk.

The picture was from the loft, one of the first ones she took of the mirror standing there.

"Notice anything weird?" Moe asked.

It took AJ a moment to realize what he was asking about.

The surface of the mirror was all gray, not reflecting the room. It was similar to how AJ had first seen the mirror, in her vision. Plus it had looked that way when she'd first pulled it away from the wall.

"That is weird," AJ said. "It must be because of the angle."

"No, because you have a second picture of the mirror and it

shows it reflecting. Taken just a couple seconds later," Moe said, swiping the first picture out for another.

"Huh," AJ said.

"What's really weird is that my pictures are the same," Moe grumbled. "The first one shows the surface as non-reflective, while in the others it looks right."

"What do you think caused that?" AJ said, sliding the tablet back across the desk to Moe.

"I have no idea!" Moe said, sounding frustrated. "I mean, if it had just been your pictures that worked that way, I might have thought you did something. But it was also one of my pictures." He paused then said, "You're the psychic. What does it mean?"

AJ sighed. She hadn't told Moe about her vision. Maybe she was going to need to do that.

"You said there was another picture that looked weird?" AJ asked.

"Yeah, the first one you took of the far loft," Moe said, swiping through shots until he found the right one.

AJ studied the picture he showed her. Light, wispy trails of...something...curled through the space.

If AJ had some sort of special effects department working for her, what she saw would be exactly what she'd want to use to show something spooky or supernatural occurring in an area.

"Huh," she said again.

"That's the only picture that shows those," Moe complained. "What did you do?"

"I didn't do anything!" AJ said. "I just took pictures. Using the camera *you* provided."

"Yeah, I know," Moe said. He shook his head. "I'm just as

bewildered as you are about these." He paused, then asked, "Are you sure you have no idea what these are?"

AJ sighed.

"You do know!" Moe pounced.

"I did have a vision about James's death," AJ slowly admitted. "The day before he died."

"Spill," Moe said grimly.

AJ paused. "As long as this conversation isn't being recorded."

Moe nodded, reached into his bag and showed her the recorder that he'd brought.

It was currently turned off.

"That's the only vocal recorder I have," Moe said.

That was the truth. AJ wasn't worried about the tablet or his phone, as she heard the truth in his voice.

So she recounted the vision, starting with how the mirror in the loft had been covered in gray mist. The people she'd seen yanked out of view of the mirror. How the far loft had appeared cloudy at first but had eventually resolved into a body, hanging, with the hair over the face so she couldn't see who it was.

Moe nodded and looked puzzled. "You couldn't see his face?"

AJ shook her head. "Nope. But I knew it was a body. And that it wasn't something I could change."

She explained how real pictures meant immutable, whereas cartoon-like images meant the future wasn't set.

"My mentor was the one who told me the difference between the two," she explained. "And no, I'm not telling you who that is, or giving you their name. Just know that they don't live here."

"Interesting," Moe said. "But you haven't had any other visions? About someone else possibly being in trouble?"

"Not yet," AJ said. "Maybe the killer just wanted to take care of James and isn't planning on attacking anyone else."

Moe nodded. "What's the timing with your visions?"

"Generally, they occur a day or two before the event," AJ said. She blinked and sighed. "I can't force a vision. I can't make it happen. I get the worst headaches if I try."

She grimaced to herself, remembering how she may have kinda, sorta, tried the previous night. And been unsuccessful.

"Have you or your crew been able to dig up anything on Kim?" AJ asked.

"It's more the absence of evidence than any evidence," Moe admitted. "Her social media pages were created only five years ago, when she moved here. And her phone, too, wasn't assigned until she moved here."

"Do you think she was someone else before then?" AJ said, confused.

"Possibly," Moe said. "Or her old page got hacked and she had to create a new one. That happens all the time too."

"Okay," AJ said. "I'm sorry I don't have anything more for you."

"Let's meet up tomorrow, compare more notes," Moe said. They made plans to meet for lunch, then Moe went on his way.

AJ tried to think after he'd gone, but honestly, she didn't have anything.

She was going to have to go and look at Kim's social media accounts later herself.

For now, she tried to put it all out of her mind and focus on the work at hand.

Chapter Eleven

Friday morning brought the rain. Not sheets of water dumping down on AJ, just a steady drizzle, almost like a heavy mist. While it was certainly colder than it had been, the rain struck her as nice, a pleasant change from the too hot days.

She knew she'd end up resenting it by the end of the season, but for now, she didn't mind it too much. Particularly since she had a headache threatening. She wasn't sure why, but it hung over her head like a dark storm cloud, making it difficult for her to think.

The tide was all the way out when she left for work. An endless stretch of sand had replaced her usual view of waves. The wind hadn't died down at all, buffeting her from the far-away water. AJ trudged up the small hill to Main Street, then went directly to the inn instead of stopping for coffee.

She was going to the Storm Brew Café for lunch with Moe. She'd get some good coffee then. In the meanwhile, she'd just make do with what Payne served at the inn.

Of course, the coffee pot in the kitchen area was empty by

the time AJ got there. Seemed there had been quite a breakfast rush, based on the number of tables still with guests eating.

AJ made a fresh pot (burning her hand in the process, because it was going to be one of those days) then bussed tables, carrying a full bucket of dirty dishes back to the kitchen.

"Where's Lola?" AJ asked Payne as he flipped pancakes on the grill.

Payne Thomas gave AJ a particularly fierce glower. "Called in sick. For the second time this week."

AJ sighed and nodded. Lola was one of Rosita's cousins, but she didn't appear to take the job too seriously. She only had a few hours in the morning, helping out with breakfast and lunch. However, this wasn't the first time she'd missed.

Payne stirred his pancake batter with vigor. AJ snuck a peek at them, but they appeared to be normal, not some strange vegan concoction that Payne was trying to slip in.

Payne Thomas was still the most handsome man AJ had ever seen—with full, black hair hanging down to the collar of his gray T-shirt, muscular arms, a wide chest, sensual lips, and a hero's cleft chin.

Despite his good looks, his crazed eyes made it impossible for her to fully trust him. He had a fervor when it came to his vegan beliefs that always set AJ's back up.

AJ rinsed the dishes, then loaded up the sanitizer for Payne, before carrying out the next order to table five.

As the café was only open until nine, and it was after eight, there wasn't a lot more for AJ to do. She still hung out for awhile, clearing tables and settling bills.

"Thank you," Payne said as he finished scraping down the grill. "I needed the help this morning. And I'll need more help at noon."

"I'll talk to Rosita about Lola," AJ promised him.

Payne stiffened and pressed his lips together for a few moments.

AJ waited to hear what he had to say.

Finally, all the tension fled from Payne's exquisite physique and he slumped, dropping his head down to his chest. "Thank you," he said softly. "I haven't wanted to say anything. I know she's going through a hard time."

"It's all right," AJ said. "You don't have to do this alone."

Payne nodded. "I was hoping I could cover for her for a while longer, but I can't. It's too much for one person."

"I can help at lunch," AJ assured him. She could postpone her meal with Moe.

"Good," Payne said. "Let me finish cleaning and start lunch prep."

AJ nodded and went back to her office, sending a message to Rosita that they needed to talk.

It didn't surprise her that just a few minutes later, a knock sounded on her office door and Rosita stuck her head in the office.

"Hola! Wanna talk?" she said with a smile.

"Yeah," AJ said.

Rosita hadn't changed much since she and her family had bought the inn. Rosita and her sister Isabell still did most of the cleaning, though in the summer they had additional family members come and help.

Rosita always presented herself as a force to be reckoned with. She was ample-sized Hispanic woman, with a thick black braid running down the center of her back. Her features were broad and spread out, with a flattened nose, fat cheeks, and a wide smile that dominated her round face. She wore a black T-shirt that morning that emphasized her curves, hanging down over sleek gray leggings.

AJ knew better than to beat around the bush with Rosita. "Lola missed her shift at the café this morning," she said bluntly. "According to Payne, it's the second this week."

That dimmed Rosita's smile. Her thick lips pressed together into a frown. "Her life, it's bad right now," she said. She held up a hand to forestall any comments. "I know. She still needed to call the family and get a replacement."

Rosita sighed, looked away from AJ, then looked back in her direction. "Have you heard of this catfishing? On the internet?"

"I have," AJ said, nodding. She'd learned a lot more about this topic just this week.

"So. She is a victim of one of those people," Rosita said. "She is afraid to leave the house."

"You heard about the person who was killed, right? James Teaford? He was a catfisher," AJ said.

"That is what set her off," Rosita confirmed. "She was a victim of his."

"Oh. Okay. But if he's gone, why is she afraid?" AJ said, confused.

"Because of that show, *Lyin' Cheatin' Stealin'.* They are in town. They've been trying to interview her," Rosita said. She sounded disgusted. "They go and knock on her door, trying to see her. Invading her privacy."

"She needs to tell them that she doesn't give her permission to be recorded. If she says that a few times, in a loud voice, they'll back down. Then she needs to say it every time she sees them. They're entertainment, not a news show, so they don't have the same protection as journalists." Or at least that was what AJ had hoped. So far, the camera people had paid attention to her requests.

"All right, I will tell her. But they will still bother her," Rosita said.

"Why?" AJ said.

"Because she doesn't have an alibi for the night of the murder," Rosita said. "The police have already asked her questions about it."

"Oh my goodness, Rosita, I had no idea! We just need to get someone into the inn as a temporary replacement. She shouldn't be trying to keep working."

"She needs the money," Rosita said grimly. "Gave too much of it to that James."

"I'm so sorry," AJ said. She sighed. "Could she work with Isabell and clean instead? While you took over the café job, at least for the first half of the day?"

Rosita blinked in surprise for a moment or so. "That might work. Make her wash sheets and towels in the basement."

AJ nodded, then felt as though she had to ask. "Did Lola have anything to do with James's death?"

"No," Rosita said emphatically. Then she sat back. "But she cannot prove it."

"I can help Payne with lunch today," AJ said softly. "Can you make sure the rest of her shifts are covered?"

"I can," Rosita said. She nodded, then stood up. "Anything more?"

"No, thank you," AJ said. "And I'm still so sorry about your niece."

"She was foolish," Rosita said harshly. "But she is still family."

AJ considered that as she turned back to her work.

Foolish. But family.

Seemed to be one of the themes of her life.

Chapter Twelve

AJ and Moe agreed to meet after lunch, at two PM, so she'd be back at the inn by three, when there would be more people checking in.

She helped Payne with lunch. They had a simple menu, a few panni sandwiches and salads. Payne offered both vegan chicken for the salad as well as cooked chicken breasts.

They never had that many people for lunch. They did have quite a few to-go orders, mostly from locals who came by to pick up something. The food from the inn offered a change of pace from the other venues in town, for people who wanted a variety.

AJ had felt a headache threatening all morning. After lunch, her entire head blossomed in pain.

This didn't feel right. It hit directly behind her eyes instead of encompassing her head.

It wasn't until AJ made it back to her office and picked up her water bottle that she realized what was occurring.

She had a vision pending.

Why was it giving her a headache? And why didn't she have a strong urge to look at water? The pull felt tenuous at best.

With a sigh, AJ locked her office door, pulled down the scrying bowl, and got her binder clips ready.

She poured water into the bowl, the gleaming light she'd been expecting suddenly spearing her eyes, making her head hurt worse.

What was going on?

AJ stared at the water, words floating from her lips.

"What can you show me? There's something to show me. Show me. Show me. I know you want to show me. Come on. Show me."

AJ had never felt as though she'd had to beg her visions to come before. But this one seemed rather reluctant.

Finally, the water in her bowl turned silver. Mists chased each other across the smooth top. Then the gray cleared.

At first, AJ wasn't certain what she saw. Was that an old-fashioned TV console? From the fifties, perhaps? The piece was large, and made out of carved wood. It held a cabinet to the left, with a large, curved TV screen to the right.

Just then, a black and white cartoon started up.

It showed a catfish, leaning back in a lounger, fishing pole in hand. Beside it, a bucket with smaller fish thrashed. Though there wasn't any sound, AJ could imagine the old-fashioned, cartoony music in the background.

The catfish caught a fish, took a look at it, then at the bucket sitting beside it, before unhooking the fish and throwing it back into the river that it had come from.

The number of fish in the bucket abruptly decreased. They no longer filled the bucket, but were now only to the three-quarter mark.

Again and again, the catfish threw back what it had caught, until just three fish remained in the bucket.

Just after the catfish had thrown its line out again, a large butterfly net suddenly appeared behind it.

With a swift scoop, the catfish was firmly caught in the net. It spasmed and tried to get away, but it was firmly caught.

All AJ could see was the catfish bouncing slightly in the net as it was carried from its lounger to a large, super-hot fire. The edges of the screen wavered from the heat.

A cast iron pan was already ready, butter sizzling. The catfish was tossed into the pan.

AJ's hand moved of its own volition, dropping a binder clip into the water, breaking the vision before AJ had to watch the catfish scream.

With a shaky breath, AJ leaned back in her chair. Her headache now bloomed not just behind her eyes but through her entire head.

This felt familiar, though. The headache and the pain after a vision. It took AJ a moment to remember.

Gladys, the ghost who had once haunted the Bridgewater Inn, had forced AJ to have a vision. Or helped her. Something. AJ's head had felt as though it was going to split apart afterwards.

Was that what was happening now? Was someone forcing her to have visions? Some invisible ghost?

"Gladys? You there?" AJ asked into the quiet of her office.

Her phone suddenly started blaring.

Great. The other ghost who occasionally haunted her had decided to speak up. Carla, who'd been an air witch.

"No one's home, something's there, but no one's home," came the refrain from a song that AJ thought she might have heard when she'd been young.

So Gladys wasn't sending her visions. Which was good, because she hadn't been around for months, and AJ hoped that the ghost had finally found her peace.

Carla wasn't claiming responsibility for it either, at least as far as AJ could tell.

However, something was there. AJ couldn't get over that. Something had "helped" her with this vision, pushing at her powers, causing her head to hurt so much as a result.

Who? Or what?

AJ had no idea.

Fortunately, she did have someone she could ask.

She sent a text to Gabby since Gabby knew a lot more about magic than AJ did. She also sent an email to Ursula, her mentor, to ask if she knew about such a thing. She had no idea if either of them knew anything, but it wouldn't hurt to ask.

It was time for her to meet with Moe. AJ forced herself up and headed out of her office. At least the day had stayed cloudy so she wasn't going to have to deal with blinding light piercing her skull, making it feel like icepicks through her eyes.

"I'll be back in an hour," AJ told Sooli, the older Asian woman who was now working the desk. She wore a beautiful tailored white blouse with an equally fine gray wool vest. Her makeup was impeccable as always, her black hair pulled back into a neat bun with two jeweled sticks holding it in place.

Sooli deliberately tugged her cat-eye glasses down with a finger. "No, you won't," she said, looking over the rim and looking like a librarian who'd just discovered spilled soda pop on a book. "You're going to whatever meeting you stupidly feel you must attend, then you're going home to rest. You look like dog poo. Am I clear?"

"But—"

"We've got it covered. Besides, you'll scare the guests looking like that. They'll think we are the home of the plague," Sooli said with a wave of her hand. "Go on now. Go pass out somewhere else."

"Yes, Mom," AJ teased.

That at least confirmed that something was going on and it wasn't all just in her head. Though the pain was at least currently all located in her head. Maybe she was coming down with something?

Relieved to have the afternoon off, even though she'd already taken off so many days that week, AJ scurried out of the inn, around the circular driveway, and headed down Main Street toward the Storm Brew Café. The cold wind actually made her head feel better. It wasn't currently raining, though she knew it would start again shortly.

She was halfway to the café when she realized that Moe was standing on the sidewalk, holding two cups of something.

"Hey there," he said as she came up.

Moe's eyes roamed over her face. He looked concerned, but he didn't say anything. "So I got you a special, and me a cup of black coffee. But I haven't drunk out of either of them, so you could have the coffee instead."

"I'm sure the special is fine," AJ said, reaching for the cup and taking a sip.

Though AJ knew, *knew* that Juli the barista didn't have magic, she'd somehow managed to give AJ the perfect cup. It wasn't coffee, but a peppermint-licorice tea that cleared out her sinuses and soothed her aching head.

"Thank you," AJ said fervently. "Is there a reason we're not in the café? Particularly in this weather?"

"There's someone I want you to meet," Moe said. He

walked down the street a ways, to his rental car, then opened the back door for her.

It wasn't until AJ had already climbed in that she realized someone else was sitting back there.

He looked young, late teens, possibly early twenties. She'd bet that he'd barely come up to her collarbone standing, though that may have just been the way he was slumped in his seat. He had stringy brown hair and an unfortunately smushed together face. His bulbous nose had zits on it and his pudgy cheeks hid dark, beady eyes. He licked his fat lips, trying to capture whatever he'd gathered there from his own cup, probably whipped cream, as he didn't quite get it all and left a faint trail of white behind.

"AJ, this is Timothy. I think," Moe said, making the introductions from the front passenger seat. "Timothy, this is AJ."

"Hi, nice to meet you," Timothy said, nodding. His voice had an unpleasant whine to it.

"What's up?" AJ said, taking her own sip of blessed tea. Her head still hurt, but the pain was easing. Slightly. Maybe she didn't have to kill herself in the next hour.

"Timothy, here, is another catfish," Moe said with a nod. "We did a show on him, what, two years ago? Exposing him?"

"Yeah," Timothy said, looking down. "And I've stopped!"

That wasn't the truth. Or it wasn't the full truth.

"Tell AJ what you told me," Moe instructed.

"I don't live here. I live up in Sunset," Timothy said, glancing over at AJ then back down. "I woke up this morning and found a noose hanging outside my backdoor."

"Ah," AJ said, nodding. Her vision was starting to make sense now. "You have, what, three people who you're still catfishing? But you've let the others go? Though you continue to troll the internet?"

It turned out that even with his pudgy face, Timothy could widen his eyes to comic proportions. "How'd you know that?"

Moe gave a very calculated chuckle. "She's a psychic."

"But you don't believe in psychics," Timothy accused Moe.

Moe shrugged. "Maybe I'm starting to."

AJ knew that he was much further along that path, but she didn't say anything.

"So now what?" Timothy asked, still whining, as if he expected them to take care of his problem for him.

"Have you gone to the police?" AJ asked.

"Yeah," Timothy said. "They know who I am, what I did. They won't help me."

AJ knew he wasn't telling her everything. It took her fuzzy brain a moment to come up with the right information.

"You went to the police in Sunset, right? How about the police here, in Milltown?" AJ said.

"You think the cops here will be better?" Timothy asked, the disbelief evident.

AJ shrugged. "It would be worth a try." She knew Officer Brendan would at least listen, regardless of Timothy's past.

"Let's go, then," Timothy said. He waved a hand at Moe. "Now."

AJ opened her mouth to complain about Timothy's assumption that either of them would help him. Then she closed it.

No, they would help him. Even though he was sort of obnoxious.

All right, perhaps a bit more than just "sort of."

Moe shook his head, threw back the rest of his coffee, then said to AJ, "I assume you know where the police station is?"

AJ grimly nodded.

Hopefully, the Milltown police would be able to do something for Timothy.

Though she knew that none of this was actually going to help her poor aching head.

Chapter Thirteen

The police station looked as ugly as it ever did, fortified against an angry mob of townsfolk that had never existed and never would. The bulletproof glass, the sturdy brick walls, the numerous security cameras—AJ couldn't get over the paranoia it showed.

The three of them walked into the station. AJ recognized the older woman who sat desk duty—Officer Toni. Her curly hair had lost more of its black and was now mostly white. She looked more like a friendly lady who would serve you tea at a cozy bookstore than a police officer. The green frame on her glasses gave her an eccentric edge, as did the thick glass that enlarged her soft brown eyes.

"Can I help you?" Officer Toni asked, as they walked up to the desk.

"We'd like to talk with Officer Brendan," AJ said.

"Let me see if he's available," Officer Toni said.

After the officer had turned to leave, AJ warned the others in a soft voice, "Whatever you do, don't accept her coffee."

"It can't be that bad, can it?" Moe asked.

"Take a deep breath," AJ instructed.

Both Moe and Timothy did.

"I see," Moe said, scenting the faint whiff of burnt coffee that always hung in the air whenever Officer Toni was in charge.

Officer Brendan came up to the front desk from somewhere in the back of the station. He had brown eyes, a perfect round shaved head and thick lips that were always smiling or looking goofy.

"Hello, AJ. Nice to see you again!" Officer Brendan said, sounding much more enthusiastic than AJ felt.

Then again, he always sounded that way. If he were a dog, he'd be a big golden retriever, full of love and possibly not the brightest pup in the pile.

Moe introduced himself, as did Timothy. From what AJ could tell, Timothy used a last name that Moe hadn't heard before.

Interesting.

"We'd like to talk with you in private for a few minutes," AJ explained.

"My conference room is yours," Officer Brendan said, leading them to one of the side rooms up front.

It was the conference room AJ had been in before, with a pale wood oval table taking up most of the center of it and chairs guaranteed to be uncomfortable scattered along the sides. It took just a few moments for them to seat themselves, with AJ and Moe sitting on either side of Timothy, almost like disapproving parents. Officer Brendan sat across from them.

"You're familiar with James Teaford, I'm assuming," AJ said.

Officer Brendan grew much more serious. "I am," he said slowly.

"Timothy was in the same line of business," AJ said bluntly. "Catfishing people. Though he's mostly stopped, ever since the show *Lyin' Cheatin' Stealin'* did an exposé on him."

Officer Brendan glanced at Moe. "That's why you seem familiar," he said. "You are not recording this, correct?"

Moe held his hands up in the air. "I am not, officer. I am not making a recording of this conversation."

AJ nodded, knowing that he was speaking the truth.

Officer Brendan stared at him for a few moments before nodding. "Good." Then he looked back at AJ. "Continue."

"Timothy found a noose outside of his back door this morning," AJ said.

Timothy took up the story when Officer Brendan turned his attention toward him. It contained a lot more details about getting up, doing some work on his computer, before finally going outside and finding the noose. He'd taken pictures of it, and showed those to Officer Brendan. A large hunk of rope had been thrown onto his roof, with just the noose dangled from it, right in front of his door. Timothy hadn't heard the rope being tossed up there—but he also admitted to sleeping with earplugs.

As far as he could tell, no one had tried to break into his house. The door had been locked and bolted, so it wouldn't have been easy to get in that way. And his windows were all shut and locked.

"I live just outside Sunset," Timothy said. "And yeah, I talked with the cops there. They wouldn't help me," he whined.

"Why is that?" Officer Brendan asked. He maintained a neutral tone, but AJ could tell that he was starting to get aggravated with Timothy.

"Because they've already had to investigate other claims

against me," Timothy said, still whining. "They're prejudiced against me."

AJ knew that there was something else there, some other history that Timothy had with the Sunset police. Officer Brendan appeared to recognize that as well, and let the complaint about his fellow police officers drop.

"We don't know if whoever threatened you was the same person who killed James," Officer Brendan said.

"It was the same person," AJ said firmly.

Officer Brendan shifted his glare to her. "Really?"

"That's my gut feeling," AJ said. She didn't want to get into anything more.

Officer Brendan sat back in his chair. "I see," he said softly. "Can you stay someplace else for now?" he asked, looking back at Timothy.

Moe jumped in. "He can stay at the inn!" he said. "The production will pay for it."

"I'm not sure that's the right place for him," AJ said slowly.

Officer Brendan nodded. "She's correct. You know about your employee?"

AJ nodded. "Yeah." She paused, then added, "Found out this morning. One of the people working at the inn has been questioned about the murder of James. She was a victim of his. She didn't do it, but I want to make sure that Timothy feels safe."

That wasn't the reason why AJ didn't want him at the inn, but she didn't need to go into just how much she instinctively didn't like or trust Timothy.

He still had people on his line. People he was exploiting.

"Fine," Moe said. "We'll find a vacation rental here. We have an agreement with a few companies. Besides, I have a couple more crew who wouldn't mind being put up someplace different."

"Wouldn't moving me here to Milltown make me more of a target? Not less?" Timothy asked.

AJ shrugged. "The killer already knows where you live. Changing residence, and staying with other people, is probably safer for you."

"Fine. I'll move. As long as the place has good internet access," Timothy said.

AJ shook her head. "You're going to have to let those three people go at some time, you know. It isn't fair to them, for you to not appear as you are."

"I'm not hurting anyone!" Timothy protested. "And I'm not taking any more money from them."

"Are you going to pay them back?" AJ said pointedly.

"I'm working on it," Timothy said begrudgingly.

That...was actually the truth.

Huh.

"I need the internet because that's still my job. I'm a Clock-Ticker influencer," Timothy said proudly. "I don't need to catfish for the money anymore."

"Good for you!" Moe said. "And it's good that you're trying to pay your victims back."

Timothy nodded. "I just get so lonely," he whined. "I need to talk to people."

"You could go and connect as yourself, you know," Moe pointed out.

AJ had the feeling that he said that line often.

Timothy shrugged.

Officer Brendan gave both Timothy and Moe his card, instructing them to let him know where Timothy would be staying so the police could keep an eye out on the neighborhood. Then he sent them on their way.

The three of them gathered outside the police station.

"Now, what?" Moe asked, glancing between AJ and Timothy.

"I'm going home. I think I may be coming down with something," she lied.

Timothy immediately spun and walked to the far side of Moe, away from AJ. "You see? This is why the internet is so much safer than meat space. No germs," he said, glaring at AJ.

"I'm sure it's not contagious," AJ said.

"Do you want a ride home?" Moe said, looking concerned again.

"Just up the street," AJ said. "Then you could drive with Timothy back to Sunset to pick up his things."

While Timothy brightened at that, Moe shook his head. "I need to make arrangements with the production company to get you a place to stay," he said. "I'll text you the address when I have it."

Moe drove back up Main Street, dropping both AJ and Timothy off close to Timothy's car.

"Are you really a psychic?" Timothy asked as they stood on the sidewalk, waiting for traffic to die down a bit so they could cross the street.

"I am," AJ said. She dragged a card out of her purse. "Contact me sometime if you want a reading."

"You do tarot card readings? How did you know about what I was doing? That I still had three people? Did the cards tell you?" Timothy asked, seeming more excited than he'd been all afternoon.

"Something like that," AJ said. They crossed the street and AJ veered off, heading toward her house.

She had a date with an ice cold pillow. And her bed. She could worry about everything else after she'd napped.

Chapter Fourteen

AJ's phone blared in the dark, waking her up. She felt around for it groggily before finally finding it. The light blinded her, sending a sharp spike through her brain.

Ugh. Just before three PM. She'd been asleep for less than twenty minutes. She needed a lot more time to recover.

"Hello, beautiful," came Roland's voice.

AJ scrunched her eyes tightly together and rubbed her forehead.

Ouch. That was a mistake.

"Didn't I send you a text, asking to postpone tonight?" AJ said.

She fumbled for the settings on her phone, finally turning it to dark mode.

Nope. The text still sat there as a draft. She had written it, but hadn't sent it.

"Uhm, no?" Roland said.

AJ stabbed the send button. "My mistake," she said. "Had a strange vision this afternoon. Can't think. Can't see. Need to sleep."

"I'll come by later," Roland said. "You don't have to see me, or spend any time with me. I'll just bring you food, drop it off and leave."

"You don't have to do that," AJ said, though that was exactly what she needed. Despite her sore head, her heart was still touched at his thoughtfulness.

"I get to take care of you when you're this sick," Roland said.

"Not sick," AJ said with a pout. "Just...vision headache. You know?"

Roland gave a soft laugh. "No, I don't know. I'm not sure anyone around here knows. I still get to worry about you, though."

"Fair," AJ said. "All right. I need to go back to sleep. How about I ping you when I wake up?"

"Sounds good," Roland said. "Sleep well. Heal."

AJ stared at the phone in her hands. She'd meant to give Roland his own key to her place. She'd just never bothered.

Maybe it was time she did that as well.

In the meanwhile, AJ trudged downstairs to change out her frozen beanbag pillow for her headache, then laid back down again, falling asleep much faster than she'd expected.

When AJ woke again, close to five PM, she felt measurably better. Her head no longer tottered as if it was in danger of falling off her neck. Or that she was going to kill herself to get rid of the pain. She texted Roland to let him know she was up, then took a quick shower to wash away some of the nap and post-headache griminess.

The water soothed her as well as the nap had, and she felt even better by the time she made it down the stairs to open the door for Roland.

He held up a to-go bag in one hand and gave her a huge

smile. He also opened up his other arm, so she could give him a hug if she chose.

AJ snuggled up to him, giving him a long comforting snuggle.

That, too, was therapeutic.

He smelled of the sweetness of just cut grass and soap and maleness and just *him*. He wore his standard gray-and-black flannel shirt, jeans, boots, and a waterproof gray windbreaker that had the name of his gardening firm on it—Jax Lawn and Garden.

"Thanks for stopping by," AJ said as she stepped back and let Roland actually enter. "Sorry about wrecking our plans for the night."

"It's all right," Roland said. "Quite frankly, I was relieved. I wasn't really up to cooking tonight anyway."

"Good," AJ said, hearing the ringing truth in his statement.

They made their way to her cozy kitchen, the pair of them easily getting out plates, serving utensils, and drinks, as Roland was as familiar with her kitchen as she was with his.

After setting everything up on the small table in the kitchen, Roland asked, "Should I talk first? Or do you want to?"

AJ breathed in the scent of the spicy *tom yum gai* Thai soup in her bowl.

"You first," she said. "And thank you again for bringing this. It's perfect."

They'd discovered that while they had different tastes— Roland preferred hoppy beer to AJ's red wine—they both considered Thai takeout to be the ultimate comfort food.

Roland regaled AJ with tales of his day, the "lovely" customer who'd tried to argue about the bill. He hadn't backed down until Roland had produced copies of the original contract showing that the customer had, indeed, agreed to everything Roland had done to his property.

Then there had been a second customer who had been much more reasonable, except that she'd wanted just a little extra when it came to every single one of Roland's services. He'd finally had to put his foot down and complain about how much those little extras were actually costing him.

AJ snorted. "Sounds like something my mom would do."

"Umm, speaking of your mother..." Roland said, letting the threat dangle.

"Oh, no. What has she done now?" AJ said.

Talking about her mother was *not* going to bring her headache back, no matter how tense she might get. Or so she told herself.

"Did your mom tell you about buying a design company?" Roland said, trying to hedge his bets.

"She did," AJ said, sighing. "Design Solutions. Let me guess. She was seeing if you wanted to work with her on retainer for the commercial side of her business."

"She didn't talk to you about this?" Roland said.

"No," AJ said, refraining from shaking her head, afraid that despite how much she was feeling recovered, she might still reactivate her headache. "That just seems to be in line with what she'd do."

"Should I do it?" Roland asked. "Should I take the job? It might turn out to be lucrative."

"I don't know," AJ said. Then she had an evil thought, and gave him a grin.

"Go on," Roland said, though he sounded cautious.

Probably wise given her look.

"Get her to send you a contract, first," AJ said. "Then go through it, or maybe have your parents go through it.

Redline it completely, and be very nitpicky about every single clause."

She didn't know if her mom would try to screw Roland over contractually.

No, scratch that.

Chances were her mom *would* try to screw Roland over via contract. Not because she didn't like him. No, because it would give him a chance to *prove* himself to her.

She was going to kill her mom one of these days.

"The contract will be mostly innocuous," AJ said after another bite of the lovely *pad thai gai* that Roland had brought. "There will be a couple of clauses in there, though, something hidden, that would trip you up. It's her way of testing you. To make sure you're good enough for me."

Roland shook his head. "That's kind of sweet, in a very twisted way."

AJ rolled her eyes. "Yeah. That's Mom."

"So how did your day go?" Roland asked.

AJ told him about the strange vision, how it had given her such a headache, her suspicion that someone or something had been there to force the vision.

"Who do you think the catfish represented?" Roland said.

"I actually met him today," AJ said. "He's another catfisher that Moe and his crew had exposed." AJ explained the rest of her afternoon, including going to the Milltown police.

"Wait a second," Roland said. "Let me see if I have the timeline straight. Timothy was threatened last night, right?"

"Yeah," AJ said slowly.

"So did you have a vision about the past? Or the future?" Roland asked.

"Huh," AJ said. "I didn't think about that."

Normally, all of AJ's visions were about future events, not

past. "Was the noose just a threat? Was the killer trying to scare him with that, and wasn't intending on killing him at that point? Will the actual attack not occur until later?"

"I don't know," Roland said. "If it was just a threat, then your vision was of the future. If the killer was frustrated in their attempt last night, then maybe you had a vision of the past. That would possibly explain the headache. You did say it didn't feel like a normal vision."

"Huh," AJ said. "That hadn't occurred to me." That explanation still didn't feel completely accurate. Possibly her vision had been of the past, but she still felt as though someone—or something—had been pushing her into it.

"Timothy should be okay though, right? Didn't you say that Moe would put him up with some of the members of his crew?"

"Yeah, he should be safer now that he's no longer on his own." AJ said, still trying to organize her scattered thoughts. "I think...I think the noose must have just been a threat. Right? Since I only see future events?"

"But it also wasn't a normal vision," Roland pointed out.

"True. So maybe the person did try to break into Timothy's house. Except," AJ paused. "The vision was all about burning the catfish. Not hanging them."

She gave a shudder. Though the vision had been soundless, she still remembered how she'd ended it before the catfish had started to scream.

Maybe it wasn't literally fire, but instead, more about torturing the catfish.

She felt like she had more questions than answers.

And she still had the sense that she was running out of time.

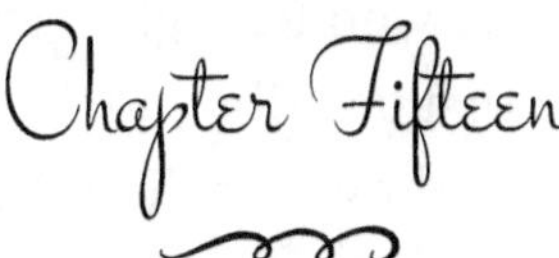

Chapter Fifteen

AJ woke up Saturday morning with Roland still there. She'd insisted, as her head was so much better than it had been. Besides, cuddles could cure most anything.

Of course, Roland had work to do that day. During the summer and the height of the season, he only took Sundays off. Even though it was already September, he still had a lot to do. He wouldn't start taking off weekends—and various weekdays—until October.

AJ didn't have clients until that afternoon, so they managed a leisurely breakfast, with Roland cooking this time, before Moe disturbed them by texting AJ.

Breaking news! You available for coffee?

AJ rolled her eyes and showed her phone to Roland.

He grinned. "Getting coffee invites from bigwig Hollywood types. I'll be able to say 'I knew her when...'."

AJ snorted. "Yeah, I don't think the star of a TV reality

show counts as a bigwig. He can't even offer me my own show."

"Really?" Roland said, tilting his head to one side and giving her a sly grin. "It kind of sounds like he already has. Wanting to meet people who have gifts, and who aren't swindling people. Doesn't that describe you?"

"This isn't a trial show for him," AJ said. "He isn't recording anything."

"Maybe he doesn't need to. Maybe he just wants to see how it goes with you. You are probably helping him shape his new show, you know."

"I didn't even think about that," AJ said.

Roland gave her a grin. "Of course not. You're much more concerned about finding James's killer. I know you, and how you get during times like these."

"Guilty as charged," AJ said. She took another sip of the delicious coffee that Roland had made and sighed.

"Duty calls," Roland said. "I have to get going anyway."

"I know," AJ said. "And I know that you'll get more days off come October. I'd like to take a weekend, or maybe a couple of weekdays, and have a getaway with you." She'd started thinking about that when her mom had sprung the girls' getaway on her and Bea.

"I'd like that," Roland said, reaching out and taking AJ's hand, giving it a soft squeeze. "Let's go someplace in November. After Halloween, and the last of the ghost tours."

"Sounds delightful," AJ said. "Let's both think about where we should go. "

"Someplace warm?" Roland suggested.

"Maybe," AJ said. "Though you know I love my ocean."

"I do," Roland said.

They said their goodbyes, and AJ walked up the short street

to Main Street, having agreed to meet Moe at the Storm Brew Café.

The weather was a typical autumn day, with cloudy skies, occasional rain squalls, the winds whipping around AJ from every direction, carrying the scent of rain. Despite it being a Saturday, very few tourists were in town. The street was practically empty.

The Storm Brew Café, however, was packed. The line was almost out the door. AJ slipped in to see if Moe already had a table.

He did. More importantly, he also had drinks in hand.

AJ stepped past the crowd, ignoring the dirty looks she got as she joined Moe at his table, at the back of the second room, in a corner, far from her usual seat near the window.

"What's up?" AJ said as she slid into her seat. "And how much do I owe you for this?"

"Depends," Moe said with a sly smile. He was wearing his usual dark-blue polo shirt and khaki slacks. "You going to tell me how you knew about Timothy still catfishing?"

AJ rolled her eyes. "Sure, but is this the right place?"

Moe glanced at the area. It was noisy in the café, and crowded. "I take your point," he said. "Where to?"

"How about the café in the inn? It'll be quiet by now. Probably," AJ said. "If it isn't, we can go to my office."

"All right," Moe said.

They stood up and wound their way outside. They hadn't gone two steps before someone had already claimed their table.

Outside, Moe slipped on a nice gray jacket with no label. AJ looked at it a couple of times before she asked, "Is there no branding on that jacket so you can wear it on TV?"

Moe nodded. "Not many people catch that. There are somethings that we can show. But frequently, yeah, we take the brand name off of things we get recorded wearing. And no, I am not recording you at this time."

AJ snorted. "And I know you speak the truth every time you tell me that."

"How do you do that?" Moe asked.

AJ shook her head as they made their way across the circular driveway of the inn. "I don't know, honestly. I think the ability came with my power. Because believe me, I was lied to all the time before."

She actually hadn't thought about her old, *old* life, back in Seattle, for a while. It felt as though so much time had passed since then, when it was only about two and a half years ago. How Ken, her ex, had betrayed her, lying to her face about where he was and what he was doing.

She'd never suspected that he was cheating on her. Not once.

She shook her head. "I wasn't able to sense people's lies right away, but the ability has definitely grown over time."

"Frightening," Moe commented.

AJ just grinned. "I don't think about it too much. Besides, people are always telling little white lies. It's the big stuff that I pay attention to." She held open one of the broad brass doors of the inn for Moe.

"Thank you kindly," he said, smiling and nodding his head.

She always loved walking into the inn, the tall ceiling in the entrance going all the way up to the second floor, the white marble floors, the glistening chandeliers. Only one couple stood at the desk, taking up Sooli's time.

AJ waved at Sooli, who shot her a glare. AJ knew she'd have to go talk with her later, reassure the older woman that she was fine. And that she wasn't actually working that day.

AJ walked with Moe to the café to the right of the reception desk. As she'd predicted, it was mostly empty, with just a single couple sitting and resting over their coffee.

To AJ's surprise, Rosita came up to their table just after they'd sat down. "We're about to close—oh. It's you."

"We wanted to have a quiet meeting here," AJ explained.

"Just don't make a mess," Rosita warned with a smile before walking back into the cooking area of the kitchen again.

"Glad to see the staff here shows you so much respect," Moe teased.

AJ snorted. "That's the owner."

"Really?" Moe said, surprised.

"Yes," AJ said. She hoped that his surprise was due to seeing the owner waiting tables, rather than because a Hispanic woman was in charge.

"So what was your big news?" AJ asked.

Moe shook his head. "You first. You are already reaping the benefits of our deal."

AJ took another deliberate sip of coffee and grinned. "What if I don't agree?" She deliberately licked the edge of the lid. "I'd always heard that if you lick it, it's yours."

Moe opened his mouth at that, then closed it again, obviously uncertain what to say.

"Let me guess. Only child?" AJ ventured.

"Yes," Moe said slowly.

"I have a younger sister," AJ said. "And possibly a bit of a rivalry with her."

"I see," Moe said, still looking hesitant.

AJ rolled her eyes and decided to put him out of his misery. She told him about the second vision she'd had, about the catfish still having three fish in its bucket, and eventually being captured and fried.

"Interesting!" Moe said, obviously fascinated with AJ's story. "And you think that the catfish in question is Timothy?"

"I do," AJ said. "I can't say for certain. But the fact that he had a lot of people on the line before, and has only kept three, and that's how many fish I saw in the bucket, makes me lean that way."

"I agree," Moe said, nodding.

"Now, my boyfriend was asking about the timing," AJ continued, deliberately mentioning the fact that she was already in a relationship.

Moe didn't react to that, so it was likely that he already knew.

AJ explained how she generally only had visions of the future, then went on to speculate that the noose probably just a threat and not a serious attempt on Timothy's life. Unless she had really seen into the past.

Moe had no answers for that, and no real way of figuring it out, short of asking the killer.

"So what do you have?" AJ asked as they wound down.

"My people found something very interesting about Kim Mayher," Moe started off with. "I told you that she didn't seem to exist until about five years ago?"

AJ nodded. "I remember that."

"Up until about five years ago, her name was actually Kim Greasewood," Moe said.

"Did she get married?" AJ asked.

"No," Moe said. "That's what I first thought. It's much more common for a woman to change her last name, even these days, so it wasn't something that stood out to anyone. No, she changed her name legally because she was a victim of identity theft. Specifically, information stolen by James Teaford."

"Huh," AJ said, sitting back in her chair. "That's interesting. Was she aware of who she was renting her property to? Or was it all managed through a third-party property management firm?" AJ knew that many of the rental properties in and around Milltown weren't actually run by the owner of the property, but by a separate company.

"We're not sure," Moe said. "We do know that sometimes she uses a management company, and sometimes she doesn't. It's almost impossible to tell based on what we can find, without doing something illegal in terms of hacking."

That actually made AJ feel better, that the production company of *Lyin' Cheatin' Stealin'* wouldn't stoop to that.

Maybe they were afraid someone would believe turnabout was fair play, and they'd be the subject of some sort of exposé.

"So what do we do next? Do we go and talk with her? Confront her about the name change, and that she actually knew James?" AJ asked.

"That was going to be my suggestion," Moe said. "I'd like you to come along, to see if she's lying or not."

"All right," AJ said. "Have you already set something up with her?"

"I wanted to check with you first," Moe said. "How about later this afternoon?"

"I have clients starting at two," AJ said. "I'm game if we can do earlier than that."

"I'll see if I can reach her and set up something earlier," Moe said, already reaching for his phone.

Moe set his phone on speaker so AJ could listen in.

"Hey Kim, this is Moe. I wanted to know if you could meet with us this afternoon, say, one o'clock?"

"What? Are you changing the time we're meeting to one?" Kim asked.

"Uhm, what are you talking about?" Moe said, confused. He glanced up at AJ, who just shrugged in response.

"Leon contacted me last night and we're supposed to meet in an hour," Kim explained.

"Sorry, sorry, he'd told me to set up the meeting, and then obviously, went ahead and did it himself," Moe said. While his voice was nice and easy, his entire body had tensed up.

"No problem!" Kim said. "Isn't that always the way with co-workers?"

"Exactly," Moe said. "So where are we meeting you again?"

"Back at the vacation rental," Kim assured him. "I figured that was better than bringing you to my mess of a house."

"Gotcha. All right! We'll see you in an hour. Bye!"

Moe heaved a heavy, put-upon sigh as he leaned back in his chair.

"Trouble in paradise?" AJ teased.

"You could say that. Look, I need to talk with Leon and find out what's going on. My car is parked just outside the Storm Brew Café. How about I meet you there in forty-five minutes?"

"Sounds great. Thank you for offering to give me a ride," AJ said.

Moe merely nodded as he stood up, phone already pressed to his ear as he headed out of the café, and probably the inn.

AJ shook her head. She wasn't certain what was going on between the two co-stars. Was it just the usual animosity? Or was there something else?

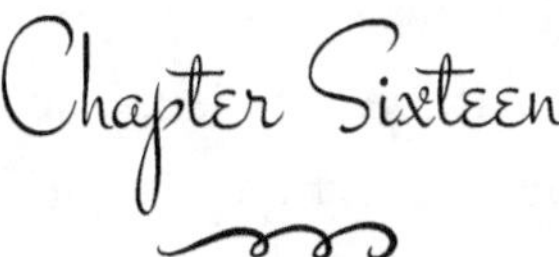

Chapter Sixteen

Pine trees pressed in on either side of the car as they drove down the dirt road, headed toward the rental. Moe had given her a fake smile when he'd met her at the car, and hadn't said anything the entire trip.

Trouble in paradise, indeed.

The entire camera crew was already at the rental, spread out, with multiple cameras, despite the ever-present threat of rain looming. Leon stood just outside the front door—still with its yellow police-tape X across it—chatting with Kim. She wore another really nice outfit—a peach colored long-sleeved shirt and beige pants, with her black gloves. AJ finally figured out that those were supposedly for arthritis.

AJ broke the tense silence. "I'm going to stay outside of camera range," she said. "I don't need to talk with Kim. I'll still know if she's lying or not. You're just going to need to ask the right questions."

"Got it," Moe said. He opened his car door, then paused. "Thank you," he said softly before he abruptly left.

AJ plastered her own fake smile on her lips as she exited the car, walking over beside the one older cameraman who'd listened to her when she'd said she didn't want to be recorded, the one who'd put down his camera first.

"Here for the drama?" he asked quietly, glancing at her then back through his viewer.

"Something like that," AJ replied, just as quietly.

"You know he's married, right?" the cameraman commented.

Huh. AJ actually hadn't gotten that feeling from him. He didn't wear a wedding ring.

"Not interested," AJ said firmly.

"Good," the cameraman said. "I'm Gary."

"AJ," she replied.

Moe hadn't confronted Leon in front of the camera. They appeared to all be good friends now, with Leon teasing Moe about being late, probably having to stop for more coffee. Moe accepted it all with a smile and a laugh that almost seemed genuine.

They were both better actors than AJ had realized. She could almost, *almost* believe their banter was real.

Only her abilities left her with the uneasy feeling that they weren't speaking the truth.

Eventually the pre-game banter wound down and Leon turned to Kim. "So, now that my co-host had graciously joined us, we have a few questions for you."

Leon glanced at Moe, who merely nodded, encouraging Leon to proceed.

"We did some digging into your background," Leon continued. "It appears that you weren't always named Kim Mayher, is that correct?"

Kim wasn't nearly as good of an actor as the two TV personalities. Her face got flushed and her smile turned icy.

"That's correct. But honestly, who would want to keep a name like Greasewood?" she said, trying to make light of it.

"But that isn't the real reason you changed your name, right?" Leon pressed.

Kim heaved a dramatic sigh.

AJ knew that if she gave that reaction the eyeroll it deserved, she'd hurt something.

"I was the victim of identity theft," Kim said. "Someone stole all my credentials. Then, they started using my name and identity to *catfish* other innocent people!"

AJ could tell the misuse of Kim's name had hurt her far, far worse than just having her identity stolen.

"I *had* to change my name!" Kim wailed extravagantly.

Moe and Leon weren't the only ones playing to the camera here.

"All these people were coming after me, accusing me of milking them out of thousands of dollars," Kim continued to vent. "And it hadn't been me! I was the victim here!"

Moe spoke up, interrupting whatever Leon had been about to say. "I'm sorry. That must have been awful."

"It was!" Kim said, tears starting to leak down her face.

AJ felt bad for her. The tears were real. The pain had been real. As was the shame of being used that way.

"Who was it that stole your identity?" Leon asked, also now starting to sound gentle.

AJ could tell he was still frustrated. He had wanted to push earlier.

"We don't know for certain. The police aren't sure," Kim said.

That was true. The police didn't know who'd done it.

"Didn't you accuse James Teaford of doing it?" Leon said, sounding triumphant.

"He's the one who started using my identity, so I always assumed it was him," Kim said. "And I was right! He all but admitted it on the show you did on him."

That wasn't exactly true. The timing didn't work out.

Fortunately, Moe brought that up. "So wait a second. You had your identity stolen five years ago. The show on James didn't air until a month ago."

"That's...that's true," Kim said, gulping and nodding. "I didn't know who'd stolen my identity. Not until I saw my picture, the old social media account I used to use, on your show. But he was the one who took it. Who stole my identity." She gulped and pressed her fingers against her eyes, trying to press out the tears. "I was a victim of his," she said softly. "That much I figured out on my own. That was why I changed my name."

"So why did you rent your place to him?" Leon pressed. "I would think you wouldn't want anything to do with him. At all."

"I didn't rent my place to him," Kim said, finally starting to sound angry.

AJ was surprised at how true that was. Kim had no idea who she'd rented to.

"When did you learn it was him?" Moe asked.

"Not until the police let me know that someone had been killed here," Kim said in a soft voice.

Moe glanced up at AJ.

She shook her head.

That had been a total lie.

"That's not quite the truth, is it?" he pressed. "You learned it was him earlier than that."

"No!" Kim said.

Still lying.

"I bet that you met him here when he checked in. Showed him all the amenities of your rental unit," Moe said.

AJ nodded. That was probably exactly what happened. Kim did have a fairly set spiel about the rental unit that she'd given Moe and her.

"I want you to leave now," Kim said. "I revoke my permission for you to be on my property. Get out of here. Now."

She turned, obviously intending on making a dramatic exit by walking into said rental unit.

However, the police tape stopped her. Instead, Kim had to pivot and stomp her way to the back of her house.

"Uhm..." Leon said, turning to Moe.

"That could have gone better," Moe said, rubbing the back of his head.

"She must have known who was renting here, and who James was, before the police contacted her," Leon insisted. "That was a good idea, saying that she knew who it was when she checked them in."

Moe shrugged. "We use enough of these units to know the drill," he pointed out dryly.

"True," Leon said. "But she was smart contacting us. We haven't been able to trace the email we got about James staying here to her."

"She used to be in IT," Moe said. "She knows how to use a VPN."

That surprised AJ. Surely someone who was in IT was smart enough to know how to protect her personal information. And to not be taken in by someone on the internet.

Right?

"A what?" Leon asked, looking adorably confused.

AJ suspected it was an act. He might honestly not know

what a virtual private network was, but the whole playing dumb and looking confused was strictly for the camera.

Moe explained some of the intricacies of networks and being able to hide your true location, also playing to the camera.

AJ remembered that was a large part of their shtick—Moe was the smart one, while Leon was the dumb one.

"So how do we break this case?" Leon said.

AJ had the feeling that this part of their conversation was entirely scripted.

"I'm going to investigate some of James's other victims, see of any of them are also in the area," Moe said with a nod.

"That's good," Leon said. "I'll keep working on Kim, and see if I can figure out her angle."

With that, the two of them nodded at each other.

"And cut!" Gary called out.

"What the hell was that?" Leon shouted, turning to Moe.

AJ was surprised at the immediate vehemence the man had on tap. He hadn't had to build up to his anger. No, he went from smiling and determined to practically screaming in point one second.

Or was this all an act as well?

"I had her," Leon continued. "Then you soft-balled her. We could have cut this segment down by a couple minutes, at least!"

Moe shrugged. "We needed to remain sympathetic here. We can go after her harder in a later segment."

"You're getting soft," Leon complained.

Moe rolled his eyes at that. "And you're getting vicious," he threw right back.

While there was some truth behind both of those statement, AJ also felt it was rote, jabs that the pair of them had exchanged so often there was no sting left to the punches.

"And what is *she* doing here?" Leon said. "Your latest fling?" he added with a smirk.

"Okay, A, none of your accusations of my supposed infidelities are true, and you know it," Moe said, starting to sound a little hot under the collar himself.

Plus, he wasn't lying. He hadn't been cheating. Possibly not ever.

"And B, she's here to help on the case," Moe said with a finality in his voice that felt real.

"Whatever, dude," Leon said. He waved a hand at Moe dismissing him before he stalked away to his car.

Moe took a deep breath, settling himself. He walked over to where Gary and AJ stood. "Was that mostly usable?"

Gary smirked at him. "Sure thing, boss. Even that end bit," he added, nodding over to one of the camerawomen who had a handheld down by her hip and was evidently still shooting.

"Great," Moe said, though AJ could tell that it was anything but. "How is the new rental working out?"

Gary gave Moe a real smile at that. "Better than the old place. I don't have to listen to Dodderman's snores anymore."

Moe snorted. "And our favorite catfisher?"

Gary sighed. "Kind of a pain, but we're working with it. Or around it. Or something."

"All right. We'll call when we have the next shoot set up," Moe said. "Thanks."

"You're welcome, boss," Gary said. He still slid a questioning eye toward AJ, but she didn't feel inclined to let him know what was going on.

They still had a killer to catch.

Was it Kim?

AJ's gut told her yes, but they needed proof.

How were they going to catch this killer?

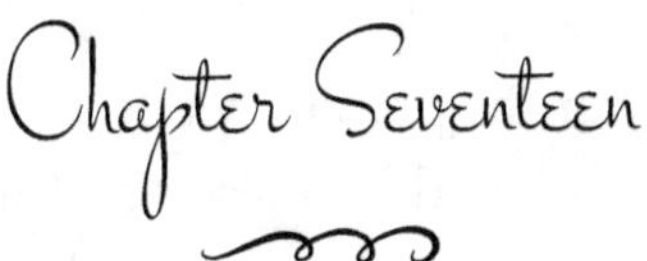

Chapter Seventeen

Moe dropped AJ off on Main Street, close to the small side street that led down to her house.

"I'll keep checking into Kim's background," he said. "There has to be some way to tie her more closely to this murder."

"I'll see if the cards can tell me anything," AJ promised as she slipped out of the car.

The rain held off until she was at the gate to her front yard, then sheets of water started pouring down. Luckily, AJ could dry herself off using magic, get the water to flow away from her, before stepping into her house.

She had a couple hours before her first reading, so she made herself a light lunch, eating in her kitchen, listening to the deluge and not thinking too hard. Afterward, she got herself a cup of her favorite peppermint-licorice tea and headed back to her reading room.

As she had some time before her first client, AJ drew the cards for herself, a three-card spread, seeing if she could figure out anything about Kim.

However, the cards seemed random to her.

The first card, representing the past, was the Hanged Man, reversed. Possibly that was how Kim saw herself, as a martyr, a victim, rather than someone gaining false intelligence or wisdom.

The next card, for the present, was the king of Swords, also reversed. A dark man with a message? But swords were all about rebirth, with all the butterflies on both the cloak of the king as well as his throne. A wrong rebirth? But Kim had chosen a new identity for herself in the past, not the present.

The future card was slightly less confusing—five of cups, not reversed. It showed a dark figure facing three cups that had overturned. Behind the person, two cups still remained upright. It was a card of loss, though something remained. In this reading, AJ felt as though the figure was ignoring a potentially brighter future, focusing instead on losses of the past. That at least felt a little right for Kim.

AJ had no idea, and swept away her cards as her first client came in.

The rest of the day flowed normally, with AJ meeting with four of her regulars, doing readings that her clients at least felt were on point. Each appointment went for forty-five minutes, giving AJ fifteen minutes in between to recover. Before the last one, she even went into the kitchen and stuck her head under the faucet.

By the end of the day, she was more exhausted than usual, and very happy that she didn't have to see anyone else that evening. The next night, Sunday, she'd have dinner with Bea and her mom, a regular get-together that they'd managed to arrange after much negotiation.

Maybe tomorrow morning she'd go swimming...it would depend on how rainy it was.

However, all thoughts of taking more time alone were banished when AJ woke up to several texts from Moe and the news that the house where Timothy and the crew had been staying had been burned down.

———

"We've got to stop meeting like this," AJ joked with Moe when he found her already waiting at a table in the Storm Brew Café.

"I know, right?" Moe said with a teasing smile. "I'm sure that the gossips have already planned our wedding."

AJ snorted. "Even though you're faithful and I'm already seeing someone?"

"You know how those Hollywood types are," Moe said with an eyeroll that even Bea would have been proud of. "Able to come in and sweep anyone off their feet."

AJ shook her head. "So what happened last night?"

Moe sighed and grew much more serious. "We think someone broke into the house. Gary woke up because he'd heard a noise. When he walked out to the kitchen, he found that someone had fiddled with the stove and disabled the pilot lights. They'd turned on all the burners to high, as well as the oven, so the stove was just pouring out gas. It was pretty noxious by the time they got everyone up and out."

"How did the place catch fire?" AJ asked, surprised at how callous the killer appeared to be, willing to kill not just Timothy but the camera crew sleeping in the rental as well.

"We're not sure," Moe admitted. "We don't think it was a random spark. It happened after everyone was outside. Maybe the killer came back? Or maybe they'd set some sort of delayed trigger? A clock with some sort of sparking device? The police are still investigating."

"Wow," AJ said, shaking her head. "That sounds pretty awful. But everyone is okay, right?"

Moe gave her a smirk. "The camera crew is a little shaken up, but fine. Timothy is threatening to sue the production company for mental anguish, claiming that none of this would have happened if he'd stayed at his house."

"Luckily, he can't prove that," AJ said. At Moe's hard stare, she amended her statement. "Can he?"

"He can't," Moe said firmly. "And the production company gets threatened with lawsuits all the time from the people we expose. So I figure they're going to hold firm and not allow him to push us around."

"Good," AJ said. "Because he *was* threatened at his home. Chances are, if he'd been there, the killer would have set his place on fire by now."

"Exactly," Moe said. He still sighed. "But Timothy is still being very whiny about the whole thing."

It was AJ's turn to roll her eyes. "Did you expect anything less?"

Moe gave a soft chuckle. "No. In all honesty, I didn't. Timothy is just like that."

"So now what? Does your company want you to pull up stakes and head out? Not continue to pursue the matter?"

"Oh no, they're all in," Moe assured her. "Gary got some really good footage of them all leaving, as well as the house exploding. The company is dying to use that."

"As long as nobody actually died," AJ said.

Moe's shrug didn't leave her with warm fuzzy feelings about the production company and who they were willing to sacrifice to put together what they considered a good show.

"So now what?" AJ asked.

"The crew have very reasonably asked that Timothy be sent

to a different rental, apart from them," Moe said. "I've pointed out that the production company isn't going to pay for it, but they're willing to pay for it out of pocket, rather than have to put up with him anymore."

"It's been what, two nights? Was he that bad?" AJ said, curious.

"You don't want to know," Moe said with a heavy sigh. "I don't blame them. This killer isn't going to stop. We're going to have to figure out how to stop them."

"First we need to know who it is," AJ said.

"Do you think it's Kim Mayher?" Moe asked point blank.

AJ reluctantly nodded. "I do. I tried doing a reading on her last night." She explained what had happened, and how the cards hadn't given her a solid conclusion.

"I have the feeling that the killer is Kim as well," Moe said. "But A, we don't know for certain, and B, we are probably going to need to catch her in the act in order to prove anything."

"Right," AJ said. "Are there any other catfishers around here? Close enough that we could direct her attention toward them? Away from Timothy, since she didn't succeed at killing him?"

"That's a thought," Moe said. "Supposedly, that's what I'm working on, though for a different angle for the show."

At AJ's questioning look, Moe said, "See if another catfisher is jealous of Timothy, or afraid that he'll expose them, like he was."

"I know you can't follow Kim around too closely," AJ said.

She paused at the look Moe gave her. "Can you? I mean, it's a small town. I think it would be difficult to follow her car, or even her person. It isn't as if there's a lot of traffic that would hide surveillance."

"True," Moe admitted. "Leon already has people on her. The problem is, his people aren't very good. She probably figured out that she was being followed by now."

"Did one of them follow her last night to the rental unit where the crew was?" AJ asked, not wanting to pursue the divide between the two co-hosts. Obviously, their animosity had been going for a while if Leon had his own people. She assumed that Moe had his own as well.

"No," Moe said with another sigh. "The detective that Leon hired—because he has a private investigator on his crew that he thinks I don't know about—signed off when Kim turned in for the night. He didn't stay outside her residence when all the lights went out and she supposedly went to bed. So we have no idea if she left in the middle of the night or not."

"And there weren't any cameras on the outside of the rental unit, showing people coming or going?" AJ said.

"There were cameras, actually. However, it wasn't until the police asked the owner for footage that we were learned they were just for show. They haven't been active in over a year," Moe said. "Mind you, when we first got the place, the reason we rented it was because of those cameras. Someone on the production crew had asked about them. But the owner lied about them working. Now, he claims that he had gotten confused, because he does have working cameras on a different property."

"So the next place you rent will have working cameras, right?" AJ said.

"Well, we were thinking about housing the crew in this inn just up the street," Moe said. "I might know someone who works there? Who might give us a deal?"

AJ paused, thinking about it. It was Sunday, and no longer high season. They would have rooms available for the week.

"But only for your crew, right? Timothy will go someplace else? I'd think he'd insist on that, as one of my staff was brought in for questioning about James's death."

"Yeah, we're still looking for a place for Timothy," Moe admitted.

"What's the next step, then?" AJ asked.

Moe shrugged. "I'm not sure. I feel as though it's two-zip, possibly even three-zip, in terms of the killer versus the good guys." He sounded defeated.

It wasn't just the case that was getting to him. There were probably other problems with Leon that were bringing him down as well.

"All right, I'll see what I can do in terms of getting the crew someplace to stay," AJ said. She held up her hand before Moe could start thanking her. "You will have to take care of Timothy, though."

"Deal," Moe said. "Thank you," he added, sincerely.

"Sure, what are potential love interests for?" AJ teased.

Moe snorted at that, and was still chuckling as they left the Storm Brew Café, him heading toward his rental car while AJ walked up Main Street to the inn, to secure some rooms for him.

She still felt as though Kim was the killer. And it disturbed her what little regard Kim had for all life.

However, what could she do about it? How could they catch her?

Fortunately, she was meeting up with some sneaky people that evening.

Namely, her mom and her sister.

Maybe they'd have an idea or two.

Chapter Eighteen

AJ finished up her story for her mom and Bea, emphasizing that she didn't know for certain if Kim was the killer. Even if Kim wasn't, how did they catch the person responsible not only for James's death, but for setting the rental on fire and nearly killing not only Timothy but the camera crew also staying there?

"Not a clue how you're going to solve this one," Mom said, shaking her head and taking another sip of the rather good red blend that she'd brought to their Sunday dinner together.

AJ snorted. "You're no help," she said. Then she looked hopefully at her sister.

Bea also shook her head. "Don't go looking at me. I'm no good at this sort of thing."

AJ hung her head in despair. "Y'all ain't no fun," she complained.

"How far back have you gone into Kim's social media accounts?" Mom countered.

AJ paused, thinking. "I haven't actually done any of that

sort of work. I've been relying on Moe and his people to do the digging."

That brought a rather impressive sigh from her mother. "You know that they're not going to do as good of a job as you are, right?"

"I actually don't," AJ said. "They get paid for doing this stuff, and they do it all the time. Right? I'd think that they'd be much more experienced and capable than I am."

"Than *we* are? No," Bea said, standing up. She had made a lovely creamy mushroom and chicken baked dish for dinner, that had been topped with biscuit halves perfectly cooked and slightly crisp. Of course, Bea had also made a side salad, but it had mostly been made up out of a very bitter radicchio. At least she'd had a strawberry vinaigrette that AJ could use to drown out the taste. (Even their mom had complained about not wanting to eat something that nasty, which had just made AJ snort and Bea roll her eyes.)

For dessert, AJ had brought a yummy lemon tart from one of the local bakeries. It had a buttery graham-cracker crust with a light lemon filling that perfectly finished off the meal.

"So let's head to the couch and start digging into Kim Mayher, AKA Kim Greasewood," Mom said, picking up her wine glass and snagging her phone from her purse.

AJ was slightly surprised at her mother's eagerness to pursue this mystery. "What happened to, 'Oh, just let the police handle it'?" she asked.

Mom shrugged as she sat down on the couch. "I know you," she said. "And I know that you won't be really good for much else until you solve this."

AJ rolled her eyes at that, but also nodded. "Roland said the same thing to me."

"Smart man," Bea said. "You gonna keep him?"

AJ paused before she answered. "Yeah," she said softly. "I think I am."

"Oh, have there been romantic developments?" Bea said, pouncing immediately. "Tell. Me. *Everything.*"

"There isn't that much to report," AJ said as she sank down on the couch, on the far side of their mom, so Bea would be in the middle. "We're just growing more comfortable, you know? And he gets me. He still prefers beer to wine," she said with a smirk. "But other than that, we're pretty compatible."

"I hear a big ol' *but* coming," Bea commented.

"No," AJ said, shaking her head. "We're just taking it slowly."

"So no progress at all?" Mom asked, scrolling through her phone, looking down and not watching AJ.

"I wouldn't say that," AJ said. "I'm thinking about giving him a key to my place," she admitted.

Mom's head came up at that, and she shared a look with Bea.

"What?" AJ asked defensively.

"I'd bet that he already had a key," Bea said.

Mom just smirked.

It surprised AJ, honestly. She would have assumed that her sister would know her better than her mother.

Then again, Bea was an admitted romantic. Mom was more practical. In that aspect, AJ was more similar to her mom than to Bea.

"So enough about me," AJ said. "We need to look into Kim's past social media accounts."

"I found Kim Greasewood on the Birdy," Mom said. "It's pretty clear where it delineated, from her posting to someone else creating the posts. The entire tone is different. She starts liking a bunch of profiles that are no longer in existence, having conversations with deleted users, and the vibe is much more sexual than it had been."

"That's kind of what Kim said, that her account had been stolen by someone who was a catfisher, who then used her profile to catfish other people," AJ said.

Mom nodded. "That fits with the profile here."

Bea started looking at Kim's old Faces account, while AJ found the account on PicturePortal, known as PP, that was primarily for sharing photos. Earlier posts were all about Kim's cats, some very nice photos of the sunset from the roof of Kim's condo in Seattle, as well as memes about how nerdy IT people were. AJ had seen most of those previously in her former life as a manager of a group of IT nerds, but she still snorted when she read them again.

Then, as her mom had noticed, the entire tenor of the account changed. No more cat pictures or funny IT memes. Instead, the pictures were primarily of women's bodies, usually with the face cropped out. AJ could tell that it was a bunch of different women, but supposedly all the sexy ones were of Kim. Plus, there were a couple of really badly edited pictures that had Kim's face pasted onto someone else's body.

AJ found it strange that someone just stopped posting on the site, and that the account was still available, that it hadn't been deleted. Maybe Kim had gotten the poster to stop, but she couldn't get the account deleted, as she no longer had access to it.

AJ went looking for Kim's current account. It had pictures of her rental units—it appeared that she had more than one in Milltown. But very few personal pictures, like her cats, or sunsets over the beach.

Maybe Kim had a different, more personal account? That this one was primarily for business?

She opened the Milltown app and started looking for someone who might be Kim, as her name wasn't listed anywhere that AJ could find.

She did find an account called BlackGloves. After perusing it for a while, she decided that it was probably Kim, as there were pictures of the same cat that had been on the PP site, before it had been taken over.

"Guys—do a search for BlackGloves, or some variation of that," AJ said as she went back to the PP site. "That's the user name that Kim has on the Milltown app."

"Found it," both Mom and Bea said at the same time.

"How did you figure that out?" Bea asked.

AJ explained about how Kim had worn black arthritis gloves the two times she'd seen her.

"Good catch," Mom said. "The account under her name is only about her rentals."

"That's what I found too," Bea said. After a few moments, she added, "Huh. Kim has a lot of quotes and memes about the importance of apologies."

"I'm actually seeing some battling memes, some about the power of a proper apology, and some about how useless an apology is," Mom replied.

AJ went and checked the Milltown app. While there weren't actual pictures of the supposed suicide note left by James, there was a report that it contained a long apology.

"Listen to this," Bea said. "'What I'd like most of all is for the one who wronged me the most to apologize for all the harms that he's caused not just me, but to every one of his victims.' Then it goes on, and actually writes out that apology."

"Not quite an admittance of murder," AJ said.

"No, but just a second," Bea said.

Bea brought up a photo and flashed it to them. "Someone

took a picture of James's suicide note and shared it. It was up for just a couple of minutes, and I happened to catch it live."

She silently handed her phone to first Mom, then AJ.

AJ read through the text of the note, then the text of the apology note that Kim had written for her betrayer.

It wasn't a word-for-word match, but it was awfully close.

"Do you think the police know about this?" Mom asked as AJ continued to look at the two texts.

"Probably," AJ said. "They might be only small-town cops, but they aren't stupid."

"However, as you said before, it's hardly an admittance of murder," Bea said.

"Can you send me that picture? Of the note?" AJ asked. "I want to forward it to Moe, see what he thinks."

AJ's phone rang within a minute of sending the picture on.

"That's it!" Moe said excitedly. "That's the smoking gun! I really don't want to ask how you got a picture of the suicide note, though."

"It was posted to the Milltown app for just a couple of minutes, and my sister managed to snag it at the time," AJ replied.

"Good. Good," Moe said. "So you didn't break into the police office and steal it. Or hack into their computers or something."

AJ snorted. "Nope. Just right place and right time." Then she sighed. "But it still isn't enough to arrest her. Probably isn't even enough to get a search warrant."

"That's okay," Moe said. "We'll come up with something. Thanks for the info though. See you tomorrow."

"I do work all day tomorrow," AJ pointed out. "But maybe we can do coffee at some point in the afternoon." Even though it was no longer season, a lot of people still checked out of the inn on Monday mornings. Plus, Rosita had asked her to also pick up a shift in the café.

"Sounds good. I'll text you tomorrow to set something up."

After AJ had hung up, she turned to see both Mom and Bea looking at her.

"What?" she asked defensively.

"Nothing," Bea said.

"Does Roland have anything to be worried about?" Mom asked, giving her a sly grin.

"No, he does not," AJ said, confused. "Why would you even ask that?"

"She doesn't see it," Bea said to Mom.

"No," Mom said, sounding thoughtful. "Interesting."

"See what?" AJ asked.

"You obviously like this Moe," Bea said.

"He's the co-host for that show. *Lyin' Cheatin' Stealin','*" AJ explained. "He's paid to be charming, and to have a lot of charisma. There isn't anything between us. We're just friends. Plus, he's married. And I have Roland."

"Right," Bea said slowly.

AJ rolled her eyes. "You're as bad as his co-host, Leon. He also accused Moe of having yet another affair, when Moe hasn't actually ever had one."

"You sure about that?" Mom said. She pulled up a news article and showed it to AJ.

The show had been on hiatus for half a year after Moe had been accused of sexual harassment.

"But look," AJ said, after scrolling to the bottom of the article. "He was cleared of all charges. The woman recanted."

"That just means the producers found her price and paid to shut her up," Mom said.

AJ was about to immediately defend Moe, but stopped and thought for a moment. "While it may be true that the producers paid her off, that doesn't mean the claims were real. Moe told Leon that he wasn't cheating, that he hadn't cheated. And I know he told the truth."

"How do you know that?" Mom asked, skeptical.

AJ paused, considering. Her mom already knew about her visions, though not her magic. The fewer people who knew that, the better.

"In addition to visions, I can generally tell when someone's telling a lie," AJ explained.

"You what?" Bea exclaimed.

"I thought I told you about that," AJ said.

Bea shook her head. "Nope."

"Crap. I didn't purposefully not tell you," AJ said.

Bea rolled her eyes. "While I might not have any special powers, and I don't always know when you're telling the truth, I think you are at this point."

AJ turned to Mom, who was giving her a calculating look. "Well?"

"I think I wish that I was younger, and that I'd managed to bring you into my business ventures sooner," Mom said.

"Mom, I'm not for hire. You can't bring me to random business meetings so I can be a human barometer for you. The whole, 'bring your daughter to work day' is no longer applicable when you daughter is older than ten."

"We would have figured something out," Mom said, still looking at her with narrowed eyes. "Can you always tell when someone's lying? Even little white lies?"

AJ shook her head. "Some people are easier to read than others. For example, Moe and Leon are difficult to read when they're on camera. They're paid to be a certain way, and it's hard to see past that façade. Most people, though, it's easy to see when it's a big lie."

She explained about Kim, and how she knew that it was James renting to her before the police had let her know about his death.

"So how do you know that she's lying? Do you have a vision or something? Do the words suddenly start coming out red? What happens?" Mom said, clearly trying to figure out how she might be able to use this new ability of her daughter's for her own personal gain.

"It's a feeling, that's all," AJ said. "It's immediate. And it's visceral, if that makes any sense. Particularly if it's a big lie. When I'm paying attention, I can also tell when someone's speaking truly."

"Hmmm," was all Mom had to say.

AJ knew better than to tell her mom to drop it.

For better or worse, her mom was probably going to include her in more of her schemes.

Heaven help whoever was currently in Mom's sights.

Chapter Nineteen

At least the Storm Brew Café wasn't that crowded Monday afternoon. Fred Hansen sat in the picture window up front, madly typing away on his laptop. A younger couple—probably tourists—sat close to the unlit hearth, both scrolling on their phones and sipping their drinks.

Moe was already there, waiting for her just inside the door. AJ went ahead and got her own coffee that afternoon, which seemed reasonable as there wasn't a line and as Moe didn't really know what it was she wanted to drink.

That day called for copious amounts of caffeine. The rain hadn't let up at all—a nice steady soaking drizzle. The temperature hadn't dropped yet, but AJ knew that fall was coming and that soon, the bone-chilling cold would arrive.

Juli gave AJ a caramel mocha with an extra shot of espresso, that had the perfect amount of flavor and zing.

Moe was looking at his phone as AJ came up and sat down. "What's up?" AJ asked.

"It's not the best news," Moe told her. He kept his eyes focused on his phone, obviously not wanting to look at her.

AJ was a little surprised at his appearance. Moe had always dressed well, with a nice shirt, some sort of pants (not jeans), and well groomed.

This afternoon, he had bags under his eyes and he looked a little disheveled when he finally did look up.

"Okay," AJ said, bracing herself.

"I've been taking care of Timothy. Put him in a temporary place last night—it was the only place we could find that was with our contracting company," Moe explained. "The production company was already bitching about putting the crew up in the inn. Though the crew volunteered to pay for it themselves, the producers are still covering it."

"So what's the problem?" AJ said. "Is Timothy going back to his place in Sunset?"

"No," Moe said. He sighed. "So I may have been keeping Leon a little out of the loop when it came to Timothy."

AJ could easily interpret that as Moe hadn't told his co-host a single thing.

"As you can imagine, he was a little pissed off when he learned about Timothy, and that we were housing him," Moe said.

AJ just nodded, encouraging Moe to continue, though dread was starting to build in her gut.

"I made the mistake of showing Leon the picture of the supposed suicide note, and then the ideal apology that Kim wrote," Moe said. "I may have wanted to show him up a little."

AJ suppressed her smile at that. Yeah, that sounded like the truth.

"So then he took over. I didn't tell him where Timothy was, but as the production company was paying for it, it wasn't that hard to figure it out," Moe said. "Leon went to see

Timothy this morning. I'm still not sure what Leon offered to pay Timothy, but it had to be massive."

"Pay him? For what?" AJ prompted when Moe didn't continue, but just stared off into space.

Moe sighed. "Paid him to agree to stay at Kim's rental. The same one that James was killed in."

"Really?" AJ said. "How—I just—really?" Why would Timothy do that?

"Yeah, really," Moe said. "It took a while for Kim to get the rental ready, get the police to turn it over to her and clean it. But as soon as Timothy was able to get checked in, the camera crew went through the entire place and set up hidden cameras."

AJ opened her mouth then shut it again. "I suppose that isn't a violation of privacy if the person agrees to it, right?"

"Exactly," Moe said. "So we have what Leon is calling a 'command center' set up so we can watch all those camera feeds at once."

AJ had visions of a van full of screens set up someplace. Surely they'd be more subtle than that?

Moe continued. "Someone will be there, twenty-four-seven, to make sure that nothing happens to Timothy. Or that the cavalry can come riding in and save the day."

"Still," AJ said, shaking her head. "Seems awfully risky."

"Leon figured it was the best way to catch Kim in the act," Moe admitted.

"Why did she agree to house another known catfisher? Surely she suspects something, some sort of trap," AJ said.

Moe shrugged. "Leon charmed her. And he can be very charming when he sets his mind to it."

"Promised her more TV time, didn't he?" AJ asked cynically.

"Yeah," Moe said with a lopsided grin. "That too."

"So now what?" AJ said.

"Now, we wait. I don't know how long it'll be before Kim acts. Will she do something right away? Or will it be a few days, when she thinks we're no longer looking, or as diligent?"

AJ shook her head. No vision was going to show her that, she was certain.

"Soooo," Moe said, hesitating before he continued, "want to meet me at the command center later tonight, just to see?"

"Sure," AJ said, though she was feeling a little cautious, particularly after the teasing that both Bea and her mom had given her.

Moe was faithful to his wife, and she was faithful to Roland. This was all just work related.

Right?

<hr>

The command center was, indeed, located in what Bea called a murder van: all black, no windows in the back, no distinguishing marks, parked in the cul-de-sac just down the road from the vacation rental.

If something went wrong, no one would be able to help Timothy in seconds. It would take minutes.

Hopefully that would be quick enough.

Moe opened the door to the back of the van when AJ walked up. She would bet that there were cameras outside of the van that let the people on the inside see who was approaching.

Hot air and the smell of fried wires wafted out at her. Possibly with an undercurrent of coffee. When she looked in, there appeared to be massive stacks of server racks on the long sides, while the far end was full of black-and-white small computer screens, each showing a separate feed with a time-stamp in the corner.

How much of the van setup was real? And how much of it was composed of props, designed to look good on camera?

"Leon wanted to set up a password for the day, secret code words for gaining access," Moe explained as he gestured for AJ to sit in the second chair in front of the screens. "We did a whole schtick that we filmed about getting into the van. But he agreed that it was just for show, and that I didn't have to make up a password every day, for every single person to enter."

"That's good," AJ said. "How would you have passed me the code? Carrier pigeon? Since I'm assuming you wouldn't want to send it to me via text or something."

"See? That's what I said," Moe complained. "Though I did suggest carrier dolphin, since we're so close to the ocean." He stopped and grinned at her for a moment. "But Leon isn't the sharpest spoon in the drawer. Calling or texting isn't secure. No matter what he thinks."

"I know the feeling," AJ said. She'd had security drilled into her head so often by her team when she'd been managing software. She wasn't as paranoid as some people—Lili, for example, not only ran her own servers but had a stupidly extensive VPN system that she used for everything—but AJ's phone was more secure than say, Bea's or her mom's.

Moe explained the setup, pointing to the various cameras. There wasn't any sound, just video, cameras set up not only in many places inside the rental, but outside of it as well.

They had a clear side-view of Timothy, who appeared to be talking to his computer. Maybe he was recording another video for his influencer channel. AJ had glanced at it, but it seemed to be full of advice that she wasn't interested in, quips about the stupidity of people, and protecting your rights against government intrusion.

He had an impressive number of followers though, over one million.

She found it interesting that the filters that he ran changed his appearance significantly, giving him a cartoon-like face. He changed his voice as well, making it sound like someone who'd sucked on a helium balloon a few minutes before. Not comically high, but still not real.

Very odd. However, it appeared to be popular.

"So, this is it?" AJ asked after a few moments.

"Yeah. Sitting here. Everyone does four-hour shifts. I'm here until midnight, then one of the crew will come in," Moe said. "Leon tried complaining about the overtime until I pointed out that someone attacked the first place in the middle of the night. We couldn't afford to not have the house covered twenty-four-seven."

"Not thrilling work," AJ admitted.

Moe just grinned at her. "I've been doing research on potential guests for upcoming episodes. As well as listening to audiobooks. 'Cause reading, well, I'd get too involved and would miss something on the cameras. That's also why the shifts are short. Too easy to stop paying attention."

AJ nodded. She could see that.

"Wanna do a reading?" Moe said, reaching for a deck of regular playing cards.

AJ considered, tilting her head to the side. She had studied a couple of systems that used regular playing cards for telling fortunes, so she had the basics down. She reached out and touched the top of the deck with a single finger.

The cards felt cold. She suspected they wouldn't respond to her at all.

"I don't think we'd get anything useful out of these," she said.

Luckily, before Moe could insist, movement caught the corner of her eye.

Timothy was standing up from behind the desk. He looked just past the camera, as if he thought it was located about three inches to the left of where it actually was. He waved, then took his shirt off.

AJ looked away. "Uhmmm," she said.

Moe was still watching the screens, his mouth hanging open.

"What's he doing?" AJ said, still not looking.

"He's getting naked. I know it isn't right to body-shame. But damn," Moe said, shaking his head. He watched for a few more moments before he told AJ, "He's gone into the bathroom."

"There aren't any cameras there?" AJ said, not daring to look.

"There aren't," Moe said. "There is a camera outside the house right next to the bathroom window, in case someone tried to break in that way. But nobody wants to see that much of Timothy."

AJ just nodded. "Timothy knows there are cameras all over the rental, right?"

"He does," Moe said. "This isn't the first time that he's, ah, *performed* for them."

AJ pressed her lips together, determined not to ask any further questions.

After a few more moments of the pair of them just sitting there quietly, AJ told Moe, "I'm going to head out for the night."

Moe gave her a bright smile. "Thank you for stopping by and seeing my new work digs."

That made AJ roll her eyes at him. She left the van, pausing to breathe in the clean night air, then starting the long trek home.

She thought about Bea and her mom's teasing earlier. There wasn't really anything between her and Moe. He hadn't tried anything inappropriate, and she wasn't tempted to either.

Yet, there was something there in their easy banter. Something that she suspected both of them recognized, but that neither of them was willing to do anything about.

Feeling more settled, she texted Roland and asked if he'd like a nightcap at her place, then smiled at his enthusiastic yes.

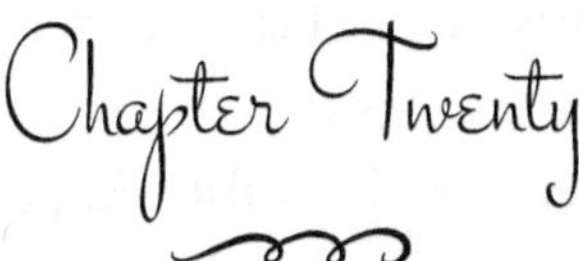

Tuesday passed with no attempt on Timothy's life, no new updates in the case, nothing out of the ordinary. AJ didn't feel like forcing a vision, and the cards told her nothing.

She tried to be relieved at a day with her normal routine, but she couldn't help but worry about the next shoe dropping.

Wednesdays were AJ's days off from the inn. During the summer she'd sometimes work weekends with Wednesday being her only day off. Now that the busy season was over, AJ not only wouldn't work weekends, but would sometimes only work on Monday and Friday, and have all the intervening days off, as well as the weekends.

Since her family was fairly small, she generally volunteered for working holidays so that others could have more time with their loved ones. This year, she'd have Thanksgiving off to spend time with Bea and her mom, but would have to work Christmas and New Year's.

So it didn't surprise AJ when her mom texted her Wednesday morning and invited her out to lunch. It hadn't been a weekly thing for them, but it had become something of a regular get-together.

They agreed to meet at Poseidon's Lair, one of the fancier fish restaurants that had a good view of the ocean. Even if that view today was somewhat spoiled with rainclouds and the tide being all the way out.

AJ braved the weather, thankful again of her ability to push the water off her body and out of her clothes when she arrived at the restaurant.

Mom, of course, had arranged a table right next to the full wall of windows looking out on the coast.

What did surprise AJ was that her mom wasn't alone. An older white man and a younger Hispanic one sat at the table to her mom's left, dressed in business casual, while the last empty seat was to her right.

"AJ!" Mom said, standing and smiling, holding her arms out for a quick hug and air kisses.

AJ obliged, suddenly understanding the performance, as that wasn't the way that they normally greeted each other.

These were backers of her mom's business. Or owners. Or someone that her mom had questions of, and she expected AJ to tell her whether they spoke the truth or not.

She was *so* going to kill her mom later.

"AJ, this is Floyd Barker and Jason Mendez," her mom said. "Their company specializes in supporting small businesses, as well as business investments."

AJ shook their hands then seated herself, pasting a smile on her face and determined to be polite.

They weren't the ones who'd ambushed her. They didn't deserve her anger. No, that was going to be reserved for the person who'd invited her.

"Irene was telling us that you run a business here in Milltown," Floyd, the older of the two, started with.

"Yes, tell him about the inn, dear," Mom instructed.

AJ felt her smile turn sweeter, the kind of look her mom said made it appear butter wouldn't melt in her mouth.

"I don't own the Bridgewater Inn," AJ demurred. "I'm just the manager there. You'd need to talk with Rosita Sanchez, as she and her family own the inn. No, I run a different small business. I'm a psychic."

Both men seemed surprised at that, the older one, Floyd, shooting her mom a confused look.

"Are you familiar with Milltown?" AJ said.

While Floyd shook his head, Jason nodded. "I grew up in Sunset," he said. "Came to visit Milltown as a kid. My aunt owned a rental here."

"You know the old Craftsman north of town, on the beach? The house that has the big sign that says *Psychic!* outside?" AJ asked.

"I do!" Jason said. "My aunt swore that Ursula, the woman who used to live there, was the real deal."

"She was," AJ said warmly. "She's my mentor, and she sold me the house on the condition that I continue with the psychic business."

"You know that isn't really legal, or enforceable," Floyd said, frowning.

"Oh, I'm aware," AJ said. She gave an actual smile to her mother. "My mom taught me contracts well. However, as I happen to be a psychic, it was nice to have an already established business to take over."

"How profitable is it?" Jason asked. He at least seemed interested, while Floyd looked as though he wanted to be anywhere but there.

"Well, I only work at the inn part-time, now," AJ said. "I used to have to work three-quarter time, but as I've grown my business, I've managed to cut down my hours and maintain the same income."

"Do you intend to ever go full time into your psychic business?" Jason said.

"I don't, actually," AJ said. "Or at least not anytime soon. I like working at the inn. I need people time, and not just people who are clients."

"I understand that," Jason said with a grin.

"At some point, sure, I'll be able to retire just on my psychic business," AJ said. "But that won't happen for quite a few years. More than a decade, perhaps."

AJ hadn't given a lot of thought to her future, but she knew that she was telling the truth. She was comfortable with her life, with working part time at the inn. She didn't feel a strong need to focus on being a psychic and giving up the rest of her life.

"Have you ever considered franchising?" Floyd said, suddenly joining the conversation.

AJ had to give him at least a B for effort.

"No, this business isn't something you could franchise," AJ said. "There aren't that many real psychics in the world."

Floyd was at least polite enough that he didn't roll his eyes at that, but AJ could tell he wanted to.

"So, are you backing my mother's business? Design Solutions?" AJ said, throwing her mother a bone.

At least her mom didn't appear to be angry at how AJ had steered the conversation, though she was certain that her mom would want to have words with her about not jumping on a potential business opportunity for the inn.

"We've talked some," Floyd admitted, giving her mom a very warm smile.

Oh.

Floyd wasn't interested in her mom's outward facing business. Or rather, not just that. He had a more personal interest in her mom.

AJ snuck a glance at her mom's face.

Huh.

She appeared to have missed that part of the conversation completely.

"Where are you based?" AJ said.

"Our office is just outside Sunset," Jason said, "though much of our business itself is online. It's actually a rare opportunity to meet with the owners we're considering doing business with."

"So what types of business services do you offer?" AJ said. May as well hear the entire sales pitch.

And judge it.

AJ and Mom stood outside the restaurant, saying goodbye to Floyd and Jason. Though Floyd looked as though he wanted to stay and chat, Jason pulled him along, saying they needed to get back to the office.

Only after they'd driven away did Mom turn to AJ, her eyes narrowed, her face frowning.

"What was that all about?" Mom demanded.

Their conversation had grown more personal than professional, though Mom had tried to steer it back a couple of times.

"Trying to judge whether Floyd would be a good match for you," AJ said with a bright, cheery smile. She was no longer angry at her mom at all for ambushing her. In all honestly it felt as though she'd been the one doing the ambushing.

"You—what?" Mom said, surprised.

"He's obviously interested in you. As a person, not just your business." AJ said. "I thought that was why you invited me to lunch with them. So that I could meet Floyd. I think he sincerely likes you."

AJ couldn't help but beam at her mom.

The lunch hadn't gone at all how her mother had obviously planned, and AJ was tickled pink at that. Couldn't wait to brag about it to Bea.

"I—that—really?" Mom said, still seemingly flabbergasted.

"Yes, really," AJ said. "Why else would you want me to meet them? You knew that they wouldn't invest in my psychic business. And you don't need them for Design Solutions."

Mom opened her mouth then shut it again. "I did want you to vet them," she said slowly, "using your superpower."

"My what?" AJ said, deliberately playing dumb.

"You know what I mean. So they were mostly honest? As honest as two people running this sort of business firm can be?" Mom said.

"They were," AJ said. "There were a few questionable moments, like when they talked about who they'd contract with to fulfill some of their services. Like, I think they have good IT and money people, but I'm not so sure about the executive side."

Neither of the two actually lied about their business. But some parts of it felt less solid than others. Half of their business was contracting out specialty services, so if a small business needed some IT, but couldn't justify a full time IT department, they could contract for one on an as-needed basis through

Jason and Floyd's business. Same with all the C-suite of executives.

"That's good to know," Mom said, still obviously thinking about Floyd. "So where are you off to for the rest of the day?" she asked as she started walking across the parking lot, heading for her own car.

"Clients later this afternoon and evening," AJ said. "No work tomorrow, so taking a day off, doing laundry, grocery shopping, like that."

"Heard from Moe?" Mom asked with a sly smile.

AJ rolled her eyes. "He and the rest of the production crew are still waiting for the killer to make a move."

"Have you had any more visions about it?" Mom said as she opened up both doors, obviously intending on giving AJ a ride home.

"Nope," AJ said. "No visions. Nothing in the cards. It's all just wait and see at this point."

"How long will they wait? The production company? Time is money, you know," Mom said. "Particularly to that type."

"Moe said they're doing research for the next couple of shows, so I think it's okay that they have some downtime right now. But they won't wait for too much longer, I suspect," AJ said.

Would Kim take the bait? Or had she decided against striking Timothy down?

As usual, too many questions without clear answers.

Chapter Twenty-One

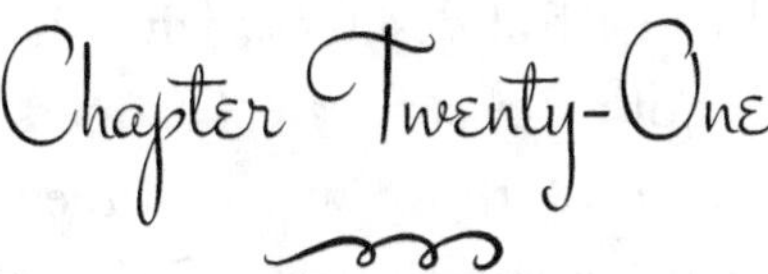

Thursday morning, Moe texted again, asking AJ to meet him for coffee. AJ readily agreed, suspecting what Moe would have to say: namely, that the production company wasn't seeing results, so they were going to close up shop.

It was a clear cold day, with blue skies and white clouds racing across it. The ocean sparkled in the distance, the tide on its way back in. AJ had no illusions about the rain being over. This was a slight reprieve, that was all.

Instead of going to the Storm Brew Café, Moe asked to meet at the internet café across Main Street from Storm Brew and a little bit further down.

AJ had been there before—they had the most wonderful maple-pecan bars, though the coffee was mediocre at best. She'd met the owners at a chamber of commerce meeting: a cute older Italian couple, who'd retired to the coast. Their son had set up the computers and ran their internet service for them.

She ordered peppermint tea and two bars from the surly

teen running the register, then picked a table at the back of the small space, as for once she'd arrived before Moe.

Just inside the door stood a dozen or so computers that people could rent. Some of them were laptops, just for email. Others appeared to be full desktops, with signs next to them detailing a long list of fancy software. Scanners and printers sat on those desks. One of those was occupied by a business-woman, scowling at her spreadsheets. Only one other table in the back was occupied, a teen doom scrolling on his phone.

Moe showed up just a few minutes later. He waved at AJ and got his own drink, then came back to sit with her. He took a sip of his coffee, then made a face as he sat down.

"That good, huh?" AJ teased. "Hopefully this will help," she added, sliding one of the plates holding a maple-pecan bar across the table to him.

He paused, taking a bite. "That's amazing," he said. He washed it down with another sip of coffee. "This, not so much," he said, indicating the coffee.

"I know," AJ said. "That's why I got tea instead."

"Locals always have the inside scoop," Moe said. "You should have warned me."

"Where's the fun in that?" AJ teased.

Moe just rolled his eyes at her before he took another bite of the bar. "You're forgiven because of this."

AJ smiled at him then looked down, taking in her own half-eaten bar. "So what's the news."

They really did have an easy way between them.

"The production company wants to pull out," Moe said. He sounded aggravated. "It's been, what, three days? And no one has made a move against Timothy."

"Do you think that it's possible the killer is just waiting for you to leave?" AJ said. "That as soon as you're gone, Timothy's dead?"

"Wouldn't be the worst thing in the world," Moe muttered. He sighed. "You know I don't really mean that. But the last couple of days have been long. Very, *very* long."

AJ nodded. She'd been expecting this news, honestly.

"Is there anything you can do to prolong your stay?" AJ asked.

"No. But...I have an idea. Leon doesn't like it, of course. However, I want to reach out to the LCS Gang, online, and see if anyone has experience troubleshooting CCTV cameras. Tell them that we're having difficulty with this surveillance."

"Have you ever done that before?" AJ asked. It was a long-shot, but maybe it would lull the killer into thinking that Timothy wasn't really being covered very well, that there were gaps that perhaps they could exploit.

"We have, actually," Moe said. He smirked. "All contact with the fandom is calculated, of course. We need to make sure that A, we don't get sued, and B, we aren't pandering to them. It's a funny line to walk."

"I bet," AJ said. "So how long before you have to pull out?"

"It's Thursday, right?" Moe said.

At AJ's nod, he continued. "We'll be here through Friday night. Possibly for half a day on Saturday. Then we'll have to pull up stakes and head out."

"If that's your timing, you really need to reach out to the community now," AJ said. "Like, get on one of those computers and do it immediately."

Moe nodded. "Kind of why we're meeting here. One of the crew gave me a script of what to say. The technical terms to use, to make it seem real and not like something I just made up."

"Right. Kim would know the difference." AJ asked. "She was in IT, didn't you say?"

"She was only sort of in IT," Moe said. "She was just in IT management, at least according to an old resume we found online. Kinda like you."

AJ blinked, a little taken aback. But honestly, what was she expecting? Of course Moe and his team would have looked into her background.

"And I'd like for you to try to have another vision," Moe continued. "See if there's something else we don't know about the killer."

"I can't force a vision," she said. "Can't will one into being."

Moe looked a bit frustrated at that. "Can you at least try?"

AJ rolled her eyes at him. "Sure, I can try. I've been trying. Nothing's been coming."

"So what does that mean? That the killer's stopped coming?"

"Or that the killer is going to stick with the same method they used previously. Fire," AJ said.

"I hadn't considered that," Moe said, his eyes wide.

AJ nodded and took another sip of her tea as a new thought occurred to her.

"Do you know what the insurance policy is on Kim's rental?" AJ asked. "Could it be that Kim isn't waiting for something on our end, but to upgrade her insurance? So she won't be out a lot of cash if the rental is set on fire?"

"I don't know," Moe said, shaking his head and snorting. "Now I understand how Leon feels, when I keep having to point out the obvious to him."

"How is Leon?" AJ asked. She hadn't really had any contact with the co-host.

"Obnoxious as always," Moe said. "I told you about maybe starting my own show, right?"

AJ nodded. He'd told her that early on, and had honestly meant it at the time. Was it still on the table?

"Seems that Leon has also read the writing on the wall, and is thinking about jumping ship," Moe said. "He might not be smart, but he isn't completely stupid. Or rather, his agent isn't dumb and is advising him. He is also planning on a new show." He grimaced.

"Do I even want to know?" AJ said, a little worried.

"True crime," Moe said, shaking his head. "He's gotten the bug of police investigations doing this piece."

"Real police work takes time," AJ said. "He'd have to be coming in after the fact and do a show about the work already done." Even in her sleepy little town the wheels of justice moved slowly.

"I told him that. He seems to think that he'll be able to wave his magical little TV remote and get things to move faster."

"How's that been working with this case?" AJ smirked.

"Not so well," Moe said. "But he's come up with a set of criteria for investigating crime in real time. Or one of his people did. It's kind of based off the parameters we use for picking guests for LCS."

AJ nodded. "I'll try to have another vision later this evening," she promised Moe. She was just going to have to be very careful about not forcing it. She didn't want to face Friday with a monster headache. "And we'll talk tomorrow."

"Sounds like a plan," Moe said, finishing off his maple-pecan bar. "Do you think you could come and sit with me in the command center tomorrow night? Come take my shift with me?"

AJ nodded. Her date with Roland wasn't until Saturday night, after the last of her clients for the day. He'd promised to take her out someplace nice.

She had a key to her house all ready for him, part of why she'd suggested going to a more upscale restaurant for dinner. She'd put it in a silver gift box with a blue ribbon on it.

"All right. I'll talk with you before then, see you around eight PM. Bring cards or something, as it'll be four hours before my shift ends," Moe said.

"You got a deal," AJ said.

"I've got a feeling about Friday night," Moe added quietly. He shook his head. "I know, I know. I'm not the psychic here. I just...I have this feeling. Something's about to happen. But not tonight. You know?"

AJ nodded. "Sometimes those gut instincts are the best guide we have."

She mused on his statements as she made her way home through the blustery winds. This wasn't the first time that Moe had talked about something almost magical happening. Like how her hand had glowed when she'd held it out to him. Or how the mirror in the rental had gone gray.

Yet, AJ hadn't felt anything magical about him.

Hopefully, though, he was correct, and they could put this all behind them tomorrow.

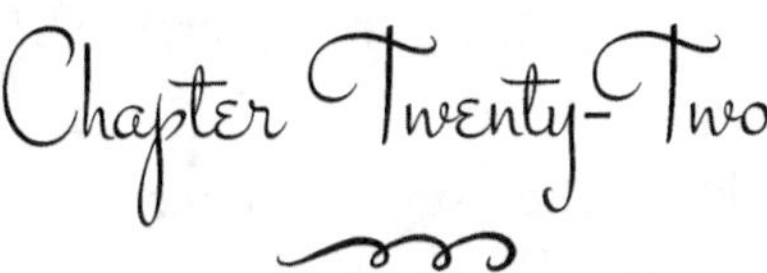

Chapter Twenty-Two

AJ sat in her reading room later that evening with a cup of tea in one hand and her scrying bowl set in front of her, fresh water resting in it. The winds howled outside, though it hadn't started raining. Yet. The air felt damp despite the wind, and AJ had put on an extra sweater, as it was that type of cold that crept into her bones.

She didn't feel the urge to have a vision. No words spilled from her lips, repetitive and almost nonsense. The reading with the cards that she'd done earlier had also been a bust.

However, she'd told Moe that she'd at least try. He'd texted a few minutes before, asking about it. She'd texted him back that she was in her reading room, about to start.

However, nothing was coming. No vision. No urging. No mists skating across the top of her bowl.

Nada.

AJ stirred her finger through the bowl of water, playing with it. The water turned as stiff as whipping cream, letting her create streaks as well as peaks and valley in it, before releasing her hold and letting the water be fluid again.

It felt good to touch the wetness. That soothed her more than the extra fuzzy warm sweater.

She honestly didn't think she'd have another vision. Kim would probably stay the course, and either move ahead with her murder plans or back off completely. AJ didn't need a vision to tell her that.

A familiar headache started encroaching across her forehead.

AJ made herself sit back from her scrying bowl.

Where had that come from? She wasn't trying to force a vision. She was just sitting there, playing with the water!

Yet the pounding in her head increased.

As did a slight—very slight—urge to see images in the water.

This didn't feel like a normal vision. No, it was more like the last one she'd had, where she could have sworn some external force was pushing the vision toward her.

Crap. She really didn't want this sort of headache. Again.

AJ jumped when her phone, sitting on the table beside the bowl, suddenly started playing an old song, something about a nowhere man. Or parts of it. The song was interrupted with static. She wasn't certain, but she thought that some of the words had been changed: instead of talking about the nowhere man being blind, she thought it said he could see through eyes not his own.

By the time the song ended, the urge to have a vision had completely dissipated. The headache had hung around, but just around the edges. It wasn't threatening to dominate the rest of her night.

AJ wasn't sure what the ghost Carla had been trying to tell her, though she had her suspicions. Instead, she texted Moe that no vision was going to come that evening and that she was going to bed.

She went into her kitchen and ran water over her head, chasing away the last of the headache.

Moe still hadn't replied when she went back to pick up her phone in her reading room. It wasn't until she was already propped up in her bed with a book that he finally replied, with just a good night.

AJ just shook her head—carefully—and went back to reading, having a very pleasant evening all on her own.

AJ juggled the coffee and chocolate-mousse tarts in one hand as she reached up to knock on the surveillance van back door with her other.

Strange. No one answered.

She was about to knock again when the door was thrust open abruptly and Leon came storming out.

He paused, looking her up and down. "Your booty call's here," he sneered.

Moe stuck his head out of the van. "Go. Just go," he instructed Leon.

"This isn't over. You can't do this to me. You'll see," Leon threatened before he turned and dramatically stomped away.

"Sorry about that," Moe said, rubbing the back of his head with one hand. "Come on in."

AJ handed Moe the bag with the tarts as she stepped up. "Do I even want to know what that was all about?"

Moe collapsed into one of the chairs in front of all the active cameras. "I told you I was looking at other opportunities, right?"

AJ nodded.

"Well, my agent called and there's a show already in development that he thinks I'd be perfect for. The host had to back out suddenly for family reasons. So I did a remote interview this morning and we're already starting negotiations," Moe said.

"Congratulations!" AJ said.

Moe held up his hand. "That doesn't mean it's set in stone. One of the old adages about Hollywood is that you never believe that something's real until two weeks after you cash the check. There are still a lot of hurdles to overcome. The network may decide at the last minute that they don't like the show. There could be some production snag. I wouldn't have a co-host anymore, and maybe after a screening, the show gets pulled because I'm not drawing in the right audience."

AJ nodded. She'd hate living in that sort of uncertainty. She much preferred having at least a bit more control over her livelihood.

Moe blew out a deep sigh. "The problem is that Leon had already interviewed for the same role. And had thought he'd got it. From what the producers have said to me, there wasn't any chance they were going to hire him."

"How did he get that so wrong then?" AJ asked. "Did he just not read the room?"

Moe had said often that his co-host wasn't that smart. However, AJ had taken that to mean book-smarts. Leon could be charming, and to do that, he'd have to be able to have some understanding of his audience.

"No, I think his agent was blowing smoke up his skirts," Moe said. "This has happened before. I've told him that he needs to get a new agent, but he's been with this agency for a long time." He shrugged. "I can't help him with this. It's a cliché but it's still really true. *Your career is your responsibility*. No one else's. No matter how much an agent supposedly will take care of you, it's still your talent and your work at the end of the day. Your paycheck."

AJ blinked, a little surprised at how intense Moe felt about this topic. She had to agree, though. "You should put that on a T-shirt. 'Your Career is Your Responsibility.' Then give it to Leon as a parting gift."

Moe's eyes got big for a moment before he started giggling. He laughed, then laughed harder. "Oh, I needed that," he gasped after a few moments. "Thank you."

"You're welcome." AJ hadn't thought her comment had been that funny, but at least Moe seemed to enjoy the snark. And he did look calmer.

"So what'd you bring?" Moe asked after wiping tears from his eyes.

"Chocolate-mousse tarts and coffee from Storm Brew Café," AJ said. "Caffeinated, as you requested." She'd gone with a decaf tea, as it was too late in the evening and she did want to get some sleep that night.

"Bless you. Thank you. Bless you," Moe said fervently.

They sat together quietly for a moment, sipping their drinks.

"Anything exciting with Timothy?" AJ said as she glanced at the various screens. Timothy was sitting at his computer recording another video.

"Nope," Moe said. "I will admit that I didn't expect him to be such an exhibitionist."

"He's desperate for attention," AJ pointed out. "That's why he did all that catfishing. So people would pay attention to him."

"True," Moe said. "But he has no shame whatsoever. You don't want to know what he's been doing on camera."

"You're right. I don't want to know," AJ said, nodding.

As soon as Timothy stood up, apparently finished recording his video, AJ turned away from the screen. "I don't need to see this, do I?"

Moe rolled his eyes. "No, you don't. It's been the exact same show for the last few nights." He waited for a few moments before he said, "It'll be safe for a while. He's taking a shower. He takes really long showers. *Really* long."

AJ opened her mouth then closed it again. She knew what men sometimes did when they took a really long shower and she didn't want to know if her assumption was correct.

"What does he do after he showers?" AJ asked.

"Goes back to his computer. Plays video games until about eleven. Then goes to sleep," Moe said.

"Can you still see into the house when all the lights are off?" AJ said.

"Nope," Moe said. "However, we have all those cameras outside, so we'll be able to see if anyone approaches." He paused, then added, "By the way, it was the outside cameras that we claimed to be having an issue with. Something about all the rain in this area." He gave her a lopsided grin.

"So if something happens, you figure it won't occur until after Timothy goes to sleep," AJ said, putting together all the things that Moe possibly wasn't saying.

"Exactly," Moe said. "But as it's only eightish now, we have a while to wait."

"Good thing I brought a cribbage board," AJ said, pulling a travel sized board out of her purse. The folded wood had gotten a little damp from the condensation of her huge water bottle that she always carried. First she wiped at the moisture on the board, then pulled out her water bottle and wiped it down as well.

Moe glanced at it. "You know, I've never seen you drink from that monstrosity," he commented. "Just coffee or tea."

"Why waste a perfectly good, hot beverage, that's already in my hand?" AJ said putting the bottle back into her purse. "I do drink from it more during the summer when it's hot," she added. Which was mostly true. The water in her water bottle wasn't necessarily for drinking. Not that Moe needed to know that.

They drew cards to see who had the lowest one and went first. He did, so she shuffled the cards and they settled in for the evening.

Chapter Twenty-Three

AJ noticed one of the camera screens blacking out. She was startled for a moment until she realized that Timothy had just turned out the main light in the rental.

"Huh. That's a little early," Moe said.

AJ glanced at one of the timestamps displayed on the screen. Ten thirty-eight. "That's good, though, right?"

"It is," Moe said. "Particularly if our theory is right and the killer is waiting for the lights to go off before they do anything. I'd been hoping all night that he'd change it up a little, and go to bed early tonight."

AJ nodded. "Has Timothy generally been on a pretty regular schedule?" she asked casually.

"Yeah. Like clockwork. Always records a video at the same time every night. Takes a shower. Plays video games, starting at nine. Has a snack at ten. Plays more video games. Goes to bed at eleven," Moe rattled off.

"Huh," was all that AJ replied, though she had a suspicion about things.

Things that Moe wanted, and put a lot of energy toward, willing them to happen.

They'd played several games of cribbage. AJ had finally agreed to up the stakes and to answer questions if she lost a game.

She'd only lost once after that, and had had to come up with questions for Moe, like the first dreams he'd had when arriving in Hollywood, what had been his most embarrassing moment on TV, and what he truly loved about his wife.

That last question had been enlightening, as Moe rambled on for quite some time about all the wonderful things regarding his spouse.

Moe, during his turn, had asked her if she'd really tried having a vision the night before.

AJ told him all about the urge and how her head had started hurting, as well as the visitation from Carla.

Then she'd had to explain more about how the ghost haunted her, using either her phone or a radio source to reach her.

Moe's eyes had gotten comically big at that. Appeared that sort of contact, like with the ghost box that Carla had used when she'd been alive, had never occurred to him before.

"How long do you think we'll have to wait?" AJ asked, glancing back toward the wall of computer screens. At least half of them had gone black as Timothy had turned out the lights.

"Not long," Moe replied. "I mean, I don't know for certain. But I can't think it'll be long."

AJ nodded and settled into wait, trying to keep her yawns to a minimum. She was up way past her bedtime, but hopefully it would be worth it. Kim would try something, and they'd stop her.

They only had to wait about fifteen minutes before AJ pointed to the screen displaying the backdoor camera. "Is that someone moving out there?"

"Maybe," Moe said cautiously.

All the cameras outside of the house suddenly turned off.

"That's our cue," Moe said. He grabbed his coat and raced out the back of the van.

AJ grabbed her purse and followed.

They ran up the short dirt drive to the rental unit. Everything was dark. Even the streetlights had gone out.

Had there been some sort of massive power outage in the area?

Wait, there was a light, moving around inside the unit. Like someone walking around with a flashlight. Was that Timothy?

Moe fumbled with the keys to open the front door. AJ dug her phone out of her purse and shook it hard twice to activate the flashlight. She shone it over his shoulder so he could unlock the door.

"Thanks," he said softly at he finally managed to get the key into the lock.

He swung the door open and rushed in, AJ on his heels.

Kim stood in the center of the open space, wearing a heavy duty mask, the kind that construction workers wore that filtered really dusty air. She looked pale by the light of AJ's phone flashlight.

Timothy lay at her feet. Had he been hit? Drugged? Was he already dead?

"I wondered how quickly you'd make it," Kim said, her voice slightly muffled by her mask. She held a flashlight in one hand, and a lighter in the other.

"What are you doing?" Moe said. He took another step forward.

"Stop!" Kim yelled. "Or this whole place goes up. Now."

"Wait, what?" Moe said.

AJ sniffed the air, but she didn't smell the awful sulfur scent of natural gas. Yet, she would still swear that there was something there that didn't belong.

She couldn't help but give a huge yawn suddenly.

Great. She shouldn't be so tired. Man, she was getting old if this was her reaction to staying up so late.

"There's enough carbon monoxide in here to stun a horse," Kim explained. "Any spark, and the whole place goes up in one huge fireball."

"Carbon monoxide doesn't burn," Moe said firmly.

"It does, actually," Kim said smugly. "Particularly when mixed with natural gas."

"But wouldn't natural gas have a sulfur scent?" AJ asked. She had gas at her house.

"The wonders of the internet!" Kim exclaimed. "You can find out how to do anything there. Including what filters to install to remove the sulfur smell of gas.""

"Don't you have detectors that would start beeping if there was some sort of gas leak?" AJ asked, finally figuring out why she was suddenly so sleepy.

"They're *supposed* to work," Kim said in an innocent voice. "How was I to know that they were defective from the factory?"

AJ knew she lied. Kim had broken the detectors, probably as part of her "prep" before Timothy moved in. And even though she hadn't actually been in IT, she probably understood how to fray wires.

Plus, if the whole place went up, there might not be enough evidence to show negligence on her part.

"So you're just going to stand there until the gas does its job on us?" Moe said.

AJ suddenly swayed. Crap. That gas was really strong.

"Either we wait until you fall down, and I blow the place up, or you rush me, and I blow the place up. You're dead regardless," Kim said. "I don't really care, one way or another. The notes I have on my computer will vindicate me. I'll still be a hero."

"But the show!" Moe complained.

"You don't care about the show. Or the LCS Gang. You were on your way out, going to another gig," Kim said.

Kim seemed remarkably well informed about what was happening. Did she have her own spy equipment on the van?

AJ slowly reached into her purse, pulling out her water bottle. As they were all standing around in the dark, it wasn't that hard to hide her movements.

"What are you doing?" Kim said, suddenly blinding AJ by shining the flashlight in her face.

"Can't I have a last drink of water?" AJ grumbled. "I'm so thirsty." Her voice sounded more dreamy than anything else right now. She hadn't planned it that way, but it worked.

"A little water isn't going to put out this lighter," Kim warned.

"Wasn't planning on that," AJ said. She glanced at Moe.

There was no helping it. She had to get them out of there.

Even if Moe was going to see things he really shouldn't.

In one fluid motion, AJ uncapped her water bottle and threw it on Kim.

She didn't use the water as a punch, to knock the other woman out, though she'd considered it. There was too good of a chance that Kim might light the lighter in her hand. Or would hit the ground too hard and something would spark.

Instead, as the water drenched Kim, it froze her. All she could do was blink in surprise.

AJ darted forward, wrapping her arms around the completely immobilized Kim.

"Grab Timothy!" she cried as panic-infused strength enabled her to lift up the woman and carry her toward the front door.

"What?" Moe said. He stayed as frozen as Kim for a moment before he hauled Timothy up, then over his shoulder in a fireman's carry. "What did you do?"

AJ didn't answer as she continued running, through the little parking area in the front of the house and onto the road. Only then did she slow down, dropping Kim to the ground and releasing her hold on the magic.

"I startled her," AJ explained as both Kim and Moe glared at her.

"You what?" Moe said, obviously not believing her.

A brilliant white light pierced AJ's eyes first, followed by a loud *whump* as the house blew up.

AJ saw the fire rushing both up and out.

Then she saw nothing.

Chapter Twenty-Four

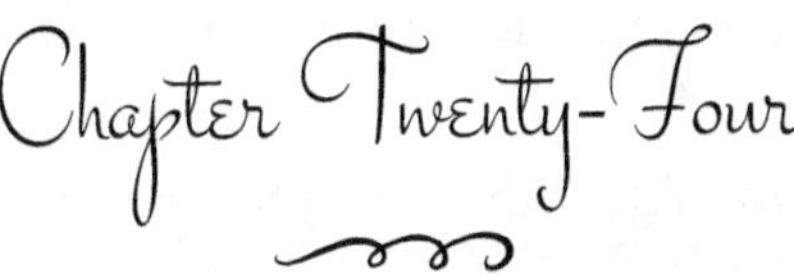

"I'll be fine. You could have taken me home," AJ assured Bea in what she hoped was a normal voice. She couldn't really tell. The blast had deafened her badly for a while, and she was only starting to get her hearing back. The ringing sound hadn't gone away, though, like someone in the next room still had an annoying alarm that they hadn't bothered to shut off.

Bea had come to get her after the EMTs and police had released her. However, instead of taking her home, Bea had tucked her away into her guest room.

"You have a concussion," Bea said patiently. "You're not going anywhere tonight. Plus, did you really want to climb those stairs up to your bedroom feeling how you do?"

AJ sighed, nodded, and winced. She wasn't thrilled about spending the night here, but then again, the thought of getting out of bed and moving wasn't appealing either. And Bea was right about the stairs going up to her bedroom. Dang it.

Everything hurt. AJ's whole body felt as though it had been run over by a truck—the power of the blast, or so the EMT had told her.

She didn't remember much either from before the house blew up as well as afterward. The EMT had told her that was normal, that people frequently lost the memory of what occurred right before a traumatic event. The brain hadn't had time to move the activities from short-term into long-term memory.

And though AJ didn't exactly remember what had happened—something with Kim and her water bottle and Moe—she still had the feeling that she really hoped Moe wouldn't remember anything either.

A muffled knock sounded on the front door.

"Oh, I hope that isn't the police," AJ groaned. She'd tried to give a statement, but it had been difficult given how her head hurt and she was never certain if she was yelling or whispering.

"You stay right there," Bea said.

Huh. Where had Bea learned such a good "Mom" voice? It wasn't as if she had kids to practice on.

"It's your internet boyfriend," Bea announced a few moments later. "Do you want to see him?"

"Sure," AJ said, though the thought of facing Moe just made her tired. "Give us a couple minutes, okay?"

Bea looked stubborn for a moment, like she wasn't going to allow AJ to see Moe, but then shook her head and walked away, as if washing her hands of the entire deal.

Moe walked into the room. He looked about as good as AJ felt, which was horrible. He had a large bandage on his left cheek where something from the exploding house had struck him. Black circles loomed under his eyes and his short hair was still a mess.

"Hey," AJ said quietly. Or at least she thought she said it quietly.

"Hey," Moe said, taking the chair next to the bed that Bea had been sitting on.

They were both quiet for a moment.

"What a night, huh?" Moe said. "Shame none of the cameras were working. We didn't get any footage of the house exploding."

"Did the crew at least get some footage of the burning house?" AJ asked. She'd been vaguely aware that the camera crew had shown up about the same time the ambulance did. The fire department had been the ones who'd arrived at the scene first.

"I think so," Moe said. "Hopefully we have enough material to put a good show together."

"Good," AJ said. "That's good." She paused, then asked, "How are you?"

"Feel as though I was run over by a truck," he admitted. "You?"

"About the same," AJ said. She only gave him a half nod, as midway through the action her body reminded her of just how dumb moving her head was.

"I just—I had to ask you. About what happened," Moe said.

AJ gave a minute shrug. "Kim blew the place up. I'm not sure how, though."

"Carbon monoxide mixed with natural gas," Moe said. "She must have fiddled with the appliances, so they were all leaking." He paused, then peered at her, eyes narrowed. "What else do you remember?"

"We got to the rental when the lights went out," AJ said. "You opened the door, and we found Kim. But it's all a blank after that."

"Really?" Moe said. "That's what you're going with?"

"What do you mean?" AJ said. "I honestly don't remember much after that."

"You don't," Moe said after a few moments. "It's really all a blank to you."

"Yeah, it is," AJ said.

"So you don't remember getting out your water bottle and tossing it on Kim?"

"I did that?" AJ said. "Why?"

Moe sighed. "So you could freeze her in place."

"She must have just been startled," AJ said, though she knew that probably hadn't been the case. She must have used her magic. The situation would have had to be pretty desperate for her to do that, particularly in front of Moe.

"Right. Let's just go with that," he said. "That is, after all, what I told the police. Not that you'd turned Kim into a living popsicle and were able to grab her, then carry her out of the house like some kind of mannequin."

AJ opened her mouth then closed it again. "I don't remember," she said again.

Moe looked frustrated. "I believe you. You're telling the truth. I don't have as good of a lie detector as you do, but I know you. You aren't lying to me. You honestly don't remember."

He looked away from her, worrying his bottom lip with his teeth for a moment, before he looked back. "The production company wants us to leave tomorrow. I have an early flight out of SeaTac."

"Okay," AJ said. "I wish you luck with your new show. You'll make it big one day, and I'll be able to say I knew you when."

Moe gave her a lopsided grin. "Yeah, well, we won't start

filming for a few weeks. Gives me a chance to recover from this," he said, indicating the injury on his face.

"So—" AJ started to say at the same moment that Moe started to speak again.

"Go on," he urged her.

"So look. It may be nothing," AJ said, still hesitant. "But I think, that while you aren't a psychic, you might have some powers of your own."

"What do you mean?" Moe said, looking thunderstruck.

"There are other abilities, beyond seeing into the future," AJ said softly. "Remember my story about the ghost who's still haunting me? Carla?"

"Yes," Moe said slowly.

"Carla advertised herself as a psychic," AJ said. "Except she didn't see the future. Her focus was on the past, with connecting people to the other ghosts still around."

"Really?" Moe said, surprised. "I guess...that makes sense. You see the future, right? It's like your specialty."

"Exactly. And some people focus on the past instead," AJ said.

"All right," Moe said. "Not sure what you're aiming at."

"There are still other people who focus on the present," AJ said. "I know someone who sees events that are occurring in the present, sometimes close, sometimes far away. I think you might have some of that skill."

"Huh," Moe said.

AJ took it as a good sign that he didn't immediately dismiss her. Then again, they were both exhausted and injured, and possibly weren't at their best.

"Remember those visions I had? How I said they weren't normal, but felt like someone was pushing them on me? I don't know for certain, but I wonder if you were the one doing the pushing," AJ said.

Moe opened his mouth, thought about it, closed it again, thought some more, before he finally said, "I really did want you to have a vision," he said. "I needed clues for what happened. But something like this has never happened before."

"I thought about that too," AJ said. "My vision of James's death happened in a mirror. Remember when we went to Kim's rental? And how the surface of the mirror was at first gray?"

"I still have those pictures," Moe said.

"That might have been a manifestation of your powers kicking in," AJ said. "But the mirror didn't have anything to show you at the time."

Moe shook his head. "I really don't know what to think about all this. What to do with it."

"There isn't anything you have to do with it," AJ said gently. "I could be wrong. However, I think you should do some experiments. See what you can manifest in the present."

Moe peered at her. "I don't know if you're saying this because you believe it, or if you're just trying to distract me from what happened just before the explosion."

AJ shrugged. "I think there's a chance you have power," she said. Then she paused. "Did the distraction work?"

Moe snorted at her. "Maybe."

Bea appeared in the doorway. "She needs her rest," she said quietly.

Moe nodded and stood. "It was lovely meeting you," he said, holding out his hand.

AJ took it. She had the feeling that he'd wanted a hug or something, but not with Bea there. Though that might not have been stopping him—she was injured, just like he was.

"Thank you," he said, squeezing her hand. "For everything."

"I'm sorry the circumstances weren't the best, but I'm glad that we met," AJ said.

"Don't be a stranger, okay?" he said with his lopsided grin before letting go of her hand and walking out the door.

Bea came back in a few moments later. "Everything okay with your internet boyfriend?"

AJ rolled her eyes. "He isn't my boyfriend. Or my internet boyfriend. Or anything else." She sighed. "He's married. I have Roland. And while there might, *perhaps*, have been something between us in different circumstances, I'm not about to be pining for him or something."

"Good," Bea said.

Despite how late it was, and how tired AJ had been earlier, she still found it a little difficult to fall asleep, thinking of what ifs.

Chapter Twenty-Five

AJ apologized again to Roland as she let him into her house. "I know this was supposed to be a night out, at a nice restaurant," she said. "But I'm still recovering."

Roland gave her a smile, then held his arms open for her so she could decide if she wanted a hug or not.

AJ snuggled into Roland. He smelled wonderful, as usual, of the conditioner he used on his beard so it stayed soft, of pine-scented cologne, and of his own, lovely masculine scent.

"Thank you," AJ said. "I needed that."

Roland nodded and put the takeout bags he held on the entranceway table. He stopped AJ from turning away, lightly touching her chin and tilting her face up. "You're starting to get a shiner," he commented.

"Yeah, the EMTs said that it's going to look as though you beat me in a few days," AJ teased.

"I'll just have to put an announcement on the Milltown app about it," Roland teased right back.

AJ smiled and stepped in for another hug. She found she didn't want to let go of him that night.

It wasn't guilt over Moe. Or at least she didn't think it was that. She'd had a traumatic experience, and she needed some stability in her life.

Something that Roland was always good at providing.

"Do we need to just go to bed and snuggle for a while?" Roland asked after a few moments.

"No," AJ said, stepping back. "I'm starving. I'm just... shaky, you know?"

Roland turned serious. "Why is that?" he asked. "Normally, you bounce back pretty quickly after a case."

AJ nodded and led the way back into her kitchen. The only lights were the ones under the cabinets, as well as a candle on the table. It was the best she could do for mood lighting.

"I don't know why this case shook me so much," AJ said. "Maybe because this one came with injuries?"

"Is that all?" Roland asked as he started unboxing the Indian food he'd brought. Though generally AJ's go-to comfort food was Thai, tonight, curry and rice had sounded better.

"Maybe," AJ said. "Maybe it was because it wasn't just me. Moe also got injured."

He'd sent a text when he'd arrived in LA, a picture of him with his arm around his wife's shoulder.

There were no what ifs, at least not for him.

"You liked this Moe," Roland said, not bothering to turn around but keeping his back to her.

Was that deliberate on his part? So he wasn't looking at her?

Maybe.

"I did," AJ said. "If he lived closer, we would have become friends." She snorted. "He's terrible at cribbage. While we were waiting for Kim to strike, we played a few games, and the loser always had to answer questions. I made him tell me about his most embarrassing moment on TV, as well as about his wife."

"He's married?" Roland said, sounding more interested all of a sudden.

AJ stopped herself from rolling her eyes at that. "Yeah. He adores his wife. Went on for almost thirty minutes talking about how great she was."

"Good," Roland said. "I'm glad." He came over with loaded plates, then looked down at the table. A small silver gift box tied with a blue ribbon sat at his place.

"What's this?" Roland asked, handing AJ her plate before moving the gift box out of the way so he could set his own down.

"It's for you," AJ said. She shouldn't be terribly nervous, but she suddenly found her hands sweating and herself a little light-headed.

Must be from the concussion.

Roland sat, the gift box still in his hand. "Should I open it now?"

"It isn't anything big," AJ said. "It's just a key to my house."

Roland smirked at her. "You know, telling me kind of ruins the surprise."

"I know, I'm sorry," AJ said. "I'm just...I'm all over the place, you know?"

"Yeah, I can tell," Roland said, setting the box to the side and reaching across the table to take AJ's hand.

"Aren't you going to open it?" AJ asked.

"I already know what it is," Roland pointed out. "And you seem as though you're kind of freaking out right now."

"I am, sorry," AJ said.

Roland shook his head. "No reason to apologize. Now, tell me what's really going on."

AJ took a deep breath and let it out slowly. "I really like you, Roland." She gave their joined hands a squeeze so he would know that she had more to say, that he shouldn't interrupt her. "I've been meaning to give you a key to my house for a while. It's just that with Ken, my ex, he defiled my house so completely. I want you in my life. I want you to be able to just stop by. But I'm still scared."

AJ found her voice dropping to a whisper as she admitted that.

Roland waited until she was obviously finished before he said anything. "I like you too, AJ. I know we've both been very careful about the 'L' word. So I'm not going to say anything like that. But I like you a lot. I'm glad you're in my life. I really don't know what I'd do if one of these cases went wrong and you were seriously hurt."

The words *or killed* echoed between them, even though Roland hadn't said them.

"How about I keep this key in my car, for emergencies only?" Roland suggested.

"No," AJ said. "You might be in your work truck, if there's actually an emergency. No, keep it on your keyring. But maybe, maybe only keep it for emergencies?" She felt bad, as if she was only giving him half a gift.

"You got it," Roland said with an easy smile. "I know you're scared. And I won't come in here unless I have your explicit permission. Like, say, you decide you want to come home to someone cleaning your house while you're out."

"You'd do that?" AJ asked, surprised.

Roland gave her a wicked grin. "I didn't say I'd be wearing any clothes by the time you got here."

AJ grinned back, her heart lighter. "So what you're saying is that you'd clean my house, but only if you could do it naked? Is that what I'm hearing?"

Roland snorted at her. "Maybe," he said, his eyes still twinkling.

AJ broke apart a piece of the garlic naan and dipped it into her green curry. It tasted heavenly, garlicy, spicy, and sweet.

"Thank you," she said after a few moments.

"Thank you for continuing to share your life with me," Roland said seriously.

The rest of the evening was spent with the pair of them cuddled up in AJ's bed, reading to each other, before AJ fell asleep in Roland's arms, finally feeling safe and secure.

Chapter Twenty-Six

Sunday night, and it was time for dinner with Bea and Mom again. Though AJ insisted she was all right, Bea still came down to pick her up and drive her up the hill, with the comment, "You look as though a strong wind would blow you over. Pack a bag. You're spending the night at my place."

With a sigh, AJ agreed. It probably wasn't the worst thing in the world for her not be alone that evening.

Though she wouldn't be drinking. Both of her eyes were starting to develop shiners, now. She was going to look like a raccoon for a week or more, even though that hadn't been where she'd gotten hit, when the house had blown up.

"You. Sit," Bea said, pointing AJ to one of the kitchen chairs while she got everything ready for dinner.

"Again with the Mom voice," AJ complained. "What is up with that?"

"I happen to have a silly older sister who's gotten into the habit of running into killers," Bea said. The words sounded light, but AJ could hear the worry behind them.

"I'm sorry," AJ said. "I really didn't mean to worry you."

Bea nodded. "I know. You're just a murder magnet, at this point."

AJ couldn't help but nod. She had seen more death since coming to Milltown than in all her forty-some years beforehand. "Why do you think that is?"

"Come to Milltown," Bea said in a radio announcer voice. "Where the water is fine, for drowning."

AJ rolled her eyes.

Mom arrived before the sisters could ding each other more. She seemed less concerned about AJ than Bea, but then again, no one would ever accuse her mother of being overly maternal. That wasn't to say that she wasn't concerned. AJ caught her mom giving her side glances every once in a while, the worry evident.

"To another successful case being closed," Bea proposed as a toast once the pot roast piled with veggies was served.

AJ raised her water glass, as it would probably be about a month before she could drink alcohol again. She clinked it with her sister and her mom.

"So what happened with Moe?" Bea asked.

AJ shrugged as she dug into the pot roast. Bea had outdone herself. Again. The meat was fall-apart tender, with a thick gravy spiced with thyme, garlic, and black pepper. The carrots and fingerling potatoes were perfectly caramelized as well.

When she finally realized that Bea had expected more of an answer, AJ replied, "He's back in LA. Back with his wife, whom he adores, by the way."

"And that's it? No more internet boyfriend?" Bea teased.

AJ sighed. "Yes. That's it. There really wasn't anything there, except camaraderie."

"That's what you kids are calling it these days?" Mom teased.

AJ rolled her eyes. "Enough about stuff that didn't happen with me and Moe," she said. "What about you and Floyd?"

Mom coughed suddenly, needing to take a large swig of her wine. "What do you mean?"

"Are you going to pursue this?" AJ said.

"Wait, what? Who's Floyd, and why am I just now hearing about this?" Bea said, glaring at AJ.

"What?" AJ said. "I'm not the one with a potential beau on the line."

Mom rolled her eyes. "It isn't anything," she insisted.

"It could be if you wanted it to be," AJ pointed out.

"So there's a man in Mom's life?" Bea said, practically purring. "Tell me more."

AJ told Bea about the lunch that she'd been invited to, making sure that they both understood that while she hadn't been thrilled about being ambushed, it had all turned out well in the end.

"So what do you think, Mom?" Bea said, turning serious.

"I know AJ thinks that maybe something is there, but I'm not sure," Mom said slowly. "No man has been interested in me for ages."

"Really?" AJ said. "Or have they been interested and you just haven't noticed? Like you didn't notice Floyd?"

Mom cleared her throat again, considering for a few moments. "I'm not saying you're right, but you might not be wrong, either."

AJ caught Bea's eye and shook her head. Given how pensive their mom had just turned, it didn't seem like they should continue teasing her about the topic.

They finished the rest of their lovely meal, as well as the delicious eclairs that Mom had brought, before settling onto the couches in the living room.

"Feels strange, no one's life or social media accounts for us to dig into," Mom teased.

"Maybe we need to start our own detective agency," Bea suggested.

"Ugh, you know what most of those private investigators do?" AJ said. "Follow people around with cameras and catch cheaters in the act. While they do good work, I can't imagine always being surrounded by the worst of humanity, always looking for bad people, you know?"

"Yeah," Bea said. "I get it. Speaking of the worst of people, that other catfisher you were using? Timothy?"

AJ nodded. He and Kim had been the least injured of the group of them.

"Seems he got scared straight by this little incident," Bea said. "He made a full apology to all the people he was stringing along, and has come out with his actual face and voice on ClockTicker."

"Good for him," AJ said. "Any news about Kim?"

"Milltown app claims that she's made a full confession. That she'd killed James, blew up the one rental, and made another attempt on Timothy. Also, she's very sorry for all the harm she's done and promises to never do it again," Mom said.

AJ didn't think she believed Kim's apology. Someone who was that callous had other issues and saying she was sorry wasn't really going to cut it. However, she also wasn't getting released from prison for a long, *long* time.

The three of them found other things to talk about—the upcoming Halloween bash on Main Street, Roland's ghost tours that would be starting soon, and the ideas Mom had for her new business (and potential business partners).

As AJ got herself ready for bed, she realized that she was

finally feeling better. Sure, she still had a concussion headache, and her body was sore, but her heart was a lot lighter.

She had friends here. A man in her life whom she adored. Family. A good job. Good clients.

A good life.

Sure, there were the occasional murders that reared their ugly heads. But she could deal with them when they arrived.

Because she wasn't alone. Not like she had been in her previous life. Not anymore.

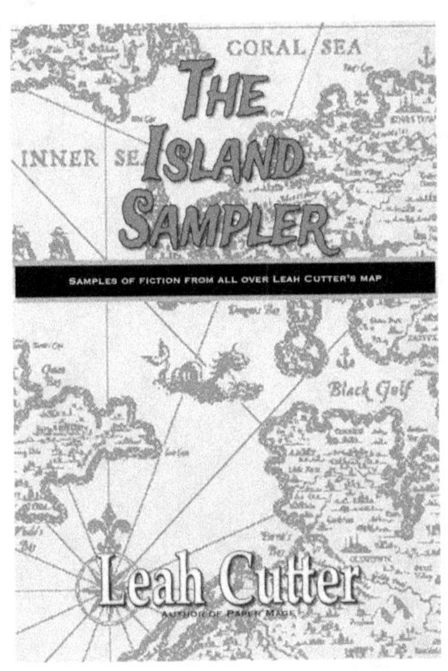

Do you enjoy exploring strange new worlds, new cultures, new people?

Journey into the various lands envisioned by Leah R Cutter.

Sign up for my newsletter and I'll start you on your travels with a free copy of my book, *The Island Sampler.*

http://www.LeahCutter.com/newsletter/

Leah Cutter tells page-turning, wildly creative stories that always leave you guessing in the middle, but completely satisfied by the end.

She writes mystery of all sorts. Her Lake Hope cozy mysteries have been well received by readers, who just want to curl up and have tea with the main character. Her Halley Brown series, revolving around a private investigator who used to be with the Seattle Police Department, leave you guessing at every turn. And her speculative mysteries, such as the Alvin Goodfellow Case Files—a 1930s PI set on the moon—have garnered great reviews.

She's been published in magazines such as *Alfred Hitchcock's Mystery Magazine* and in anthologies like *Fiction River: Spies*. On top of that, Leah is the editor of the quarterly mystery magazine: *Mystery, Crime, and Mayhem*.

Read more books by Leah Cutter at www.KnottedRoadPress.com.

Follow her blog at www.LeahCutter.com.

Read more mysteries at www.MCM-Magazine.com

Reviews

It's true. Reviews help me sell more books. If you've

enjoyed this story, please consider leaving a review of it on your favorite site.

Come someplace new...
Do you enjoy exploring strange new worlds, new cultures, new people?

Journey into the various lands envisioned by Leah Cutter.

Sign up for my newsletter and I'll start you on your travels with a free copy of my book, *The Island Sampler*.

http://www.LeahCutter.com/newsletter/

Buy More!
Did you know that you can buy directly from the Knotted Road Press website?

https://www.knottedroadpress.com/shop/

About Knotted Road Press

Knotted Road Press publishes dynamic fiction set in exotic locations. Our authors cover a wide range of genres including science fiction, fantasy, mystery, literary, and poetry. We also have unique non-fiction voices in genres such as autobiography, business, cookbooks, and how-tos. We offer both DRM-free ebooks and print books for a global readership.

Knotted Road Press
www.KnottedRoadPress.com
www.KnottedRoadPress.com/Shop

www.ingramcontent.com/pod-product-compliance
Lightning Source LLC
Chambersburg PA
CBHW071434100726
47908CB00004B/1152